After Battersea Park

Jonathan Bennett

RAINCOAST BOOKS
www.raincoast.com

Raincoast Books acknowledges the ongoing support of the Canada Council; the British
Columbia Ministry of Small Business, Tourism and Culture through the B.C. Arts
Council; and the Government of Canada through the Book Publishing Industry
Development Program (BPIDP).

First published in 2001 by

Raincoast Books
9050 Shaughnessy Street
Vancouver, B.C.
V6P 6E5
(604) 323-7100

www.raincoast.com

1 2 3 4 5 6 7 8 9 10

Canadian Cataloguing in Publication Data

Bennett, Jonathan, 1970–
  After Battersea Park

  ISBN 1-55192-408-0

  I. Title.
  PS8553.E534A73 2001   C813'.6   C2001-910221-6
PR9199.3.B37795A73 2001

Cover photograph by Jonathan Morgan/Stone
Printed and bound in Canada

After Battersea Park

For Wendy

Contents

The two brothers walking hand in hand back up along
the Barranugli Road did not pause to consider who
was who. They took it for granted it had been decided
for them at birth …

— Patrick White, *The Solid Mandala*

The words I knew said Britain, and they said America.
But they did not say my home. They were always and
only about someone else's life.

— Dennis Lee, *Body Music*

PROLOGUE

The first two streaks of light separate and float across the surface of the sky. Noah's been out here before. In the dark. Alone.

He is paddling to an outer reef, accompanied by seagulls, hovering, floating. His surfboard is long and white with a single fin. As a young Hawaiian, he used to make this paddle in no time. Now, almost thirty years later, it's taking much longer.

His strong, brown arms pull him through the water in alternating strokes; he feels the quiet thump of his board on the chop. The taste of the sea is in his mouth. Farther out the waves pitch over the shallow reef, crack as they land. The offshore wind blows spray back from the waves' lips in a fan of mist lit by new cuts of crimson light bleeding into the dark sky.

Beneath him a school of fish, shimmering silver.

His father had been right. He'd have an hour out here before he needed to be at the hotel, behind the bar at work, slicing up lemons, scratching at the dry salt on the skin of his arm.

Alongside the reef he feels the waves as they break, grinding the bare coral. After the sets roll in off the horizon, they end their journeys here in a single, almighty heave. Here waves turn themselves inside out, a single moment of harmony at the break-up of their existence. It is a moment that cannot be witnessed so much as experienced. For surfers this is a secret spot discovered through heredity.

Noah takes the drop. Fifteen vertical feet, sliding to rails, a bottom turn carve — the marble sea. Below him flashes of reef colour the half-light. Spectres of sea life fork through the wave like veins; his fingers dig into a wall of surging blue, arcing above him; his knees bend so that his head clears the pitching barrel. He straightens up, then slouches; he's inside, alone, surrounded by water, in the hollow home where echoes quiver forever.

He stretches out his arms in a cross, but he can't touch either wall. He is centred in the deep, long ride. He is alone.

He is in a park, long ago. Against the dirty grey London sky, a white woman clutches a brown-skinned man. They are whispering.

Please don't. Don't.

It is a moment in suspension.

Don't. I'll fix it. I promise.

In the park, families, couples, old men and children conduct their lives in full view, knowing their secrets are safely hidden away.

The woman runs her hand across the man's cheek, his face in anguish. Small drops of rain begin to fall and they grasp each other, attempt to conceal their faces from the twins — not quite four years old — each boy clinging to a leg. It's a game in the beginning: each parent's limb the unmovable trunk of a tree. They laugh as they weave in and out of a private forest, gleeful at the lack of objection from their mother and father. Suddenly, the twins sense a change in the weather.

Two little dark heads, identical light brown faces, look up.

Two women appear. They remove the first woman from the man; they take the twins. The man is left standing alone in the park, his head lowered against the oncoming rain.

Noah opens his eyes and the water is a mirror. He is beside his reflection. He bows his head, cuts back, blasts the lip, turns,

turns again, and then flies away into the offshore spray, into the air like a seagull. For a moment he sinks, his feet touch the coral. Then he is back up into the wind and onto his board, paddling out to another wave, another rush, another birth, another chance to live, to father, to husband, to imagine a future for himself in a way that is not the way it really happened.

PART I

Margaret's flat was one of three on the ground floor of an old sandstone mansion that looked out across Sydney harbour. Standing in the lounge, Curt remembered the day his mother moved in, years ago, when he had still been a teenager.

Look at that view, Curtis. This is divine.

The two of them had sat on the floor eating fish and chips, planning where they would put the furniture. He had crossed and re-crossed his long brown legs, uncomfortable, while his mother drank gin and tonics from a paper cup.

Do you think the bed would fit under the window, Curtis? Help mummy move it. She loves to wake in the morning sun.

At his new school the next day, the finality of his parents' divorce — the rip and tear of it — had hit him hard. Playing cricket, batting, he'd taken an uncharacteristic prod at a ball well outside the off stump and dragged it on. An inside edge. The wickets had splayed open and the ball rebounded and hit him in the head. Out for only two runs. He'd walked back to the small pavilion with sweat stinging his eyes, a raw throat and an egg swelling under his cap. It seemed like such complete loss.

Now, years later, his mother was dead.

It was a different sort of loss now, Curt thought. He sat at her old piano and ran his hands over the keys — the sharps, flats and naturals. Everything she owned was still in its place. Now, looking at something (a book on a shelf, put there by his

9

mother), the logic of his adult years fell away, paralyzing him. What if someone was to move it?

He'd not slept well for the past two nights, unable to relax, to let go and slide into sleep. Perhaps, he thought as he pulled the stool out from under the piano, he was afraid of what he might dream.

Curt laid his fingers on the correct keys and played the first bars of *The Skye Boat Song*. It was one of the few pieces his mother could play from memory; it was enough to conjure up her slender white fingers. More than the gin or the anger, this sad song she'd sung to him as a little boy, stroking his brown cheeks, his fine dark hair, *this* was his mother.

It was quiet now. She lingered about him, a weakening shadow. Beside the front door, her brown gardening shoes, heels touching, toes slightly apart, were unlaced and ready. Curt swung around on the piano stool. Her flat, her home — the smell of the lemon wood polish, the colour and order of the book spines; the Jacobean sideboard where each Christmas Eve he would open the cutlery drawer, scoop up fistfuls of inherited silverware with yellowing bone handles and set the holiday table; the oil painting of a Scottish castle, the gold-framed mirror in the foyer, all of this had been hers. Until three days ago.

In truth Curt felt his mum might come through the door with armfuls of fruit and booze any minute, saying, "Oh, darling, I was getting grog, and then I went to the green-grocer's. Sorry I'm running late." Surely it had all simply been a misunderstanding.

As the sun sank closer to the horizon, the sky faded off into a dark metallic blue. Out in Sydney harbour, the reflections of silver boats bobbing on their moorings crisscrossed the water.

The sound of cicadas swelled in the late afternoon air. Curt stretched out across his mother's bed and took the envelope from his pocket, unfolded a thin sheet of pale blue airmail paper:

Darling heart:

When I first brought you home, you were my jewel. I was so undeserving of your love. For months I feared your real mother would come for you, wanting you back. But I earned you, didn't I darling? Didn't I sing to you? Hold you? Didn't I protect you? We used to be inseparable, you and I.

I am so sorry for this. But you'll forgive me. I promise.

You'll always be my love, my dearest, Curtis.

— Mummy

Curt studied each word. Each letter cleanly executed. He stared at the *M* beginning *Mummy*. Upper case. She had never capitalized it. In a shoebox somewhere, he must have an old Christmas card with "love, mummy" on it as proof. This *M* was the *M* of her name, her signature. Had she begun to sign her name and then stopped? Had she not been his mother in the final moments before her death?

Twenty-seven prescription sleeping pills and a stomach full of gin. Her resolve, steadfast to the end. She lay dead for twelve hours before Curt's aunt, Jilly, found her slumped in her chair. Not late for tennis but dead.

Curt folded the note and placed it back in the envelope. He gazed at the ceiling, his eyes following the Art Nouveau loops and swirls dancing down the lead-lined windows, the exposed Balmain sandstone walls, the wide wooden floor-boards, the door handles that looked like claws, the near-circular archway, the lip of the verandah framing the harbour

as it stretched out to the heads, over open ocean first reaching
Fiji, then Hawaii, San Francisco, Toronto, London, Madrid,
Bombay, Darwin, across the outback deserts, home again to
Sydney and under the lip of the great curved verandah, right in
behind his eyes, into his own, blessed darkness.

"Wake up, Curt. You can't stay here again tonight." Kylie.
Curt hadn't heard her enter. He'd been asleep. Finally. "Why
don't you just come back to Coogee. Stay for a few days," she
added as he struggled to open his eyes.

He looked at her. He couldn't isolate a single emotion.

"Ah. Ciggy? Wanna ciggy?" Kylie nodded and walked
toward the verandah.

Outside they stared down Rose Bay and Vaucluse, middle
harbour, and across to Manly, the sky and water an identical
blue. In front of them, tiny and alone, slept Shark Island.

"It's what Australia is to the Yanks or even the poms," she
began.

"What are you talking about?" he said.

"Symbolically, I mean. Shark Island is Australia," she continued, unperturbed. "There we are. A sparsely populated
island, vaguely exotic, dangerous sounding, but to the world
at large ultimately insignificant. Australia as defined through
foreign eyes." Kylie lit a cigarette. Curt wasn't responding. As
she inhaled, she ran her fingers along the grooves in the Celtic
weave carved into one of the sandstone columns.

"You should come back to Coogee, Curt."

"I don't live there anymore, remember?"

"You didn't officially move out." Silence. "Have you spoken
to your father?"

"I went down to Dad's this morning. He's moving tomorrow. To the North Shore. He's got dodgy timing."

"Look, with all of this ... your mother ... do you ..." She paused to inhale. "Would you like to get back together? At least until you get past this? Curt. Come home with me."

"No. I need to stay." He did not look at her. He did not get up when she did.

Half an hour later, Curt slowly moved to the kitchen, unscrewed the top off the gin bottle and raised the rim to his lips. His eyes watered, his hands felt clammy. He grabbed a tumbler and poured four fingers over ice. He crossed the room and plunked the glass down on the piano's polished top.

He began quietly, in the key of A minor, then louder, drifting into E minor. Soon he was pounding out chords more church music than jazz. He forced himself to flatten the notes, play more lightly. He modulated into G, played a ninth and an odd version of an old blues tune he'd not thought of in years. His right hand never left the keyboard; his left brought gin to his mouth. When a new melody began to take shape, he snatched a piece of manuscript paper, scribbled down a chord progression . . . notes intersected, bouncing off one another, looping back, relaying, racing, seducing. He developed a new counterpoint progression, one hand on the keyboard, the other scribbling. The notes hung in the air, drifted. He placed his index finger on the D, gently suspending it, an afterthought. Music that spoke the sentiment of the moment or undercut it.

Curt was writing faster than he ever had before. Since he had read his mother's letter, her oddly shaped M, he'd felt the music inside him, note after note, falling from his hands. Suddenly his reflection in the piano's dark lacquer stopped him. The curve of his mouth, a ring of condensation from the glass, he drew the arc of his smile, went farther to mark out the line of his jawbone, the bridge of his nose, the outline of his eye, the furrows of his brow. He finished the gin, crushed the ice between his teeth and went to look for his car keys.

Curt stood in the doorway of Kylie's flat. He still had a key. A black T-shirt, a pair of socks and his old jeans remained on the floor where he'd left them a week ago. His boxes were piled at the door. He'd done a half-hearted job of packing, unsure if the decision was final or merely intended to provoke.

Kylie was out. He fell into the loveseat, a little drunk, the final moments of sunset filling the room with a tungsten light, as in a flashless indoor photograph. An old jazz standard swam in his head, a repetitive baseline, an alto sax. Stillness descended. He seemed to be on the verge of recovering something lost, a memory perhaps, a face.

When Kylie came home, they ate pizza from Giovanni's, drank a beer and made love. Sitting up in bed, Curt hummed a few bars of something. Kylie told a long story about her co-workers involving a colleague, her boss and a misunderstanding. There was a punchline. Curt incorporated his laugh into his hum. Nothing and everything had changed.

They slept without touching until Curt woke, tears rolling onto Kylie's breasts. Her fingers ran through his dark, shoulder-length hair, stroked his cheek and forehead, whispered the string of words she'd learned would soothe and heal.

They slept this way, Curt in Kylie's arms, his eyes tender for a time from the dry, sea-salt air.

William found his landlady's kitchen uncluttered and in good order. At first Janis was simply an older woman who waved to him in the mornings as he left for work. She drove a messy, old vw that sat in the driveway — a carcass of a car. He'd been inside her living room too, which doubled as a den, only last weekend. Everywhere he'd looked there were open books, outspread newspapers, dog-eared magazines, yellow sticky notes, grapefruit shells, half a dozen unframed prints, pen lids, pop cans, CD cases.

Yet now, looking into her kitchen, William found that her chic, glass-fronted cupboards exposed tapered plate stacks and earthenware coffee mugs in height-conscious rows. Hanging over the sink, her copper pots descended in order of capacity, and her spice jars were full and labelled in careful handwriting. He *recognized* her handwriting. Perhaps he was familiar with her flowing upper-case *G* and minimalist lower-case *m* from the crossword they'd worked on together.

"Stay and help me. It'll help pass the time while I paint my nails," she'd said.

With wet polish and bits of Kleenex wedged between her toes, she'd insisted on doing the writing. They had disagreed for a quarter of an hour over nine-down.

Or did his familiarity with her handwriting come from the not-so-subtle reminder she'd left him soon after he'd moved in?

William, don't forget to take your GARBAGE to the curb tomor-
row. If you don't, I'll know you had fish for dinner last Tuesday.
Thanks, Janis.

Peeling sweet potatoes, Janis hummed something William recognized but couldn't place. An airy folk song, a difficult
soprano melody that begged the harmony now accompanying
her in his head. A sheet of newspaper caught the peels as they
fell. Janis worked slowly, the knife sliding along under the skin
toward her thumb. William knocked gently on the doorframe.

"Oh, hello, William, I didn't see you there."

He entered, prompted by her smile. Janis' thick, grey-
brown hair hung straight down her back.

"I heard you singing," he said. "My window is open."

"What can I do for you?"

"Just wanted to drop off the rent cheque."

Janis rinsed her hands under the tap, shaking them, reaching for a towel. "Have you eaten?" She took cheque from his
hand, then placed it on top of the fridge.

"Ah, no. Not yet."

"Can you join me for lunch? Soup. Homemade."

"Great," he said. He put his hands in his pockets, fidgeting,
his face suddenly itchy. He'd forgotten to shave.

Janis plopped the sweet potatoes and peas into a pot,
adding stock and other ingredients he couldn't make out. She
wore a pair of faded men's jeans. Her waist was slighter than
he expected, but her hips were … practical. She'd kicked off
her sandals in the middle of the floor so that her bare feet piv-
oted and slid across the ceramic kitchen tiles. Her tendons
tightened, her toes curled and fanned as she shuffled from one
cupboard to another. Her nails were painted a rusty red and as

she bent down for a pot from a low drawer the cuff of her jeans lifted slightly and he caught a glimpse of a fine silver anklet.

William stretched his hands across the table in front of him, his fingertips running along the grooves of the old pine boards, separating and spreading with age. Janis parcelled up her newspaper and peels, gave the pot a swift stir and joined William at the table. The kitchen walls were washed in the faint glow of sunlight

"It's a harvest table, an antique. My mother gave it to me. It's from our family's cottage, up north."

"Get up there much?"

"In the summer mostly. It's not winterized. The soup will take about half an hour. I have to gather together a manuscript I was editing. Someone's coming round to collect it. Shall I turn on the radio?"

"Why don't I come back later. I didn't mean to impose."

"No, stay. You shouldn't spend a day like this in the basement. Look, the crabapple tree is beginning to bloom."

He turned and looked outside at the tiny bursts of crimson dotting the tree where only last week there was snow.

"We get grapes too. It's delicious in the summer. You'll like it," she said as she wandered into the living room.

Classical music filled the kitchen with strong, triumphant notes. Janis returned with a newspaper and the manuscript. "I can sort through this stuff here. Shall I open a bottle of something?"

While William sipped his wine, he remembered the three weeks in March he had walked the streets surrounding the university, then down into the old Italian neighbourhood. He had ventured farther north and west before he'd finally found the sign for a basement apartment in Janis' house. They had been cold, dark days, his hands thrust deep inside his pockets, his heart heavy. April had, at long last, made him leave. After five years.

Even though it was a basement, William had loved the apartment on first sight: big, lots of light and a garden. He hadn't wanted to be this close to the noise of Bathurst Street or even St. Clair Avenue (the house was only a few streets southeast of the intersection, and he could still hear the faint bell of a streetcar), but he had liked the feel of the place, liked the old walls and the windows and the red bricks. Besides, he'd known he was running out of time. He'd handed Janis cheques for first and last months' rent and moved in the next day.

His mother, Ruth, had driven in from the suburbs to lend a hand, but Janis had been the one who helped him carry his futon down the back stairs.

"Your mother?" Janis had wondered aloud when a very pale-looking woman pulled up in front of the house.

He'd smiled. "Yes. I'm adopted."

Now Janis looked up from her work. The music bubbled and simmered around them. *Four Seasons*, Vivaldi. I thought it appropriate."

He said nothing.

"You must think I'm a sad old cliché." Janis served the soup. "Is toast okay?" she asked. She blew on her soup. "There's pear in it."

They ate in silence, had another glass of wine, a cup of coffee.

Janis opened the old leaded window and took a cigarette and lighter from her pocket. "I read something interesting in the *Globe and Mail* this morning. As an artist, you might enjoy it." She fumbled around behind her chair, looking for the newspaper. "As a rule," she began, filling the pause in conversation, "I don't smoke inside, only when I have guests. You don't smoke, do you?" She glanced over to where she'd been peeling the sweet potatoes. The remaining sections of the newspaper were folded on the counter.

"No," he said.

"My ex-husband didn't smoke either. Although I'm told he does now, which is odd, don't you think? To start so late in life?"

"Yes, I suppose it is."

"Robin and I were married for almost twelve years. He's an antiquarian book dealer. His shop's down by the university. He left me for a history professor: Dr. Ann John." Janis exhaled, the smoke splitting the rays of sunlight coming in through the window. "Compact, mean little name. Ann John. All those Ns. He's a bastard."

William pressed his lips together.

"Oh, sorry, listen to me going on," she mumbled and collected the newspaper. She read several paragraphs aloud before giving up and began to paraphrase. "It goes on to talk about modern art and how it's disintegrating, literally, in the museums. Apparently the materials new artists use were not made to last. Quite a problem the curators say."

"A blessing in some cases if you ask me," he said, smiling.

With lunch over, Janis suggested they start another crossword. "I'm supposed to be editing a speech for ..." she hesitated "... a local politician."

"Who?"

"Rather not say."

"Why not?"

"He's very conservative. Artists don't typically approve ..."

From opposite sides of the table, they leaned in, pondering this week's clues under the waning influence of the white wine, the wash of blue light and Vivaldi. William studied her handwriting. Her hands. Wrists. Forearms. Shoulders. Neck. Mouth. Lips.

"Do you have any kids?" he asked.

"No. Robin and I had always planned to, but …"

Her eyes were blue. Light blue.

Aunt Jilly appeared through the back door and stood before Curt in an aqua dressing gown.

"You okay?" Curt reached out to touch her shoulder, but she fell into his chest. Her narrow body heaved, and he couldn't remember ever having felt her breasts against him. He had never looked down at the crown of her head, never seen her brown hair giving way to light grey roots and white scalp. She gripped handfuls of his T-shirt, holding herself upright.

Jilly's house backed onto the playing fields of the private boys' school Curt had attended after he moved to Sydney's eastern suburbs with his mother. During his first year at the school, sitting on the grassy hill with his new mates at lunchtime, he used to look over at this house, its bricks smooth and coloured a dark chocolate-brown, almost black.

As always the lawn was trim, the tiled path swept, the hedge squared. The morning sky was a clear blue — the moon was still out. An outside toilet sat at the end of the garden path, which detoured to avoid the old outstretched rotary clothesline. These luxuries helped to date the house, as did the coarse buffalo grass and the huge oak tree.

After a minute she managed, "I'm sorry, Curt." He walked her to the back verandah where she collapsed into a wicker chair.

Curt warmed the teapot and watched Jilly on the verandah through the window. She had never married. She taught at a local primary school and she'd moved back into this house, alone, when her father died some years ago. Jilly had always been on the periphery of Curtis' life, standing toward the back of every family photograph. She'd given him socks and undies for Christmas every year, practical, spartan. For birthday lunches she'd take him to The Garden Restaurant in the Botanical Gardens, a tradition a dozen years running. They'd sit upstairs on the balcony with the wisteria creeping about them, the purple blooms, and look out over the velvety park and gardens, at the pond, the ducks. Jilly loved cricket as much as Curt did, so they rarely talked of other matters.

Although Curt was still reeling from Aunt Jilly's sobbing, he prepared himself to broach the topic of his mother's service.

He poured her tea and, without meaning to — indeed, he had every intention of asking something direct, clear and personal — he asked what the overnight score in the Perth test match was. They both seemed incapable of talking about the only subject, the only person, on their minds. Neither knew how to start, so neither did for a time.

April Tanaka was not at the old apartment on the day William went back to collect his few remaining things.

"I'm going up for one last look," William told Francisco as he slammed the sliding door of his boss's van. It was cold in Toronto but not snowing.

It looked like *he* would be moving in soon. Nathan. A man he had welcomed into their lives, as his friend. Innocently. But April had always been right there.

He imagined Nathan, making small talk, cracking smooth jokes, as he carried boxes up the stairs. What would go through Nathan's mind when he saw William's old, leftover labels on the storage boxes, legible but fading, written back when he and April had moved into this place together. Would he feel like a victor, or a replacement.

Look for a new place, William. This was over long before I finished it. The time has come to actually do something — you've always hated that.

William slid the key from his ring and placed it on the table, the table April had painted, the table he had bought from a junk shop two summers ago. The long wall where his posters, artwork and photographs had hung looked grey even though he had painted it a cold white. The back of his mouth burned, his eyes grew heavy.

William fumbled around for a pen. Lipstick on the mirror appealed to his state of mind, but reason got the better of him, and he glanced at the phone instead. After dialling their number and being bumped into voice mail, he left his final goodbye after the beep, after his own voice inviting friends and strangers to *leave a brief message after the tone.*

"It's me," he announced. "I've done it. I'm gone."

First he poured two brimming glasses of Shiraz.

"Cheers, I guess," said Curt. Kylie raised hers carefully and nodded a little.

Then garlic, basil, olive oil, oregano, fusilli, crushed plum tomatoes, a baguette, a blues album, candle wax running along the table in a slow, thick stream, cards, black coffee, port, Coltrane, bed.

Through the open window, the sound of the shore breakers, mixing with the threads of laughter from the Coogee Bay Hotel only blocks away, drifted in. Unable to sleep, Curt got up and leaned into the window frame; the sea spread out before him. The lights of tanker ships lined the horizon as Kylie slept on, her chest rising and falling beneath a white sheet. He began writing notes and bar lines and time signatures.

He'd not discussed his day with Kylie, the hours he'd spent with Jilly that afternoon when they'd finally moved beyond cricket and ventured through the thick silence to her memories of the years shared between she and his mother.

"I loved Margaret as a sister," she had said finally. She'd reminded him of the time when his mother and father had divorced, how she'd taken Margaret in, supported her. She had spoken quietly, sipping her tea.

At first, Curt had felt like a gossip, a traitor. Had it been right to talk about his mother like that? Yet remarkably he'd felt buoyant as his memories composed, the pieces falling together, childhood pictures reordering and refocusing themselves.

When he'd left they'd hugged, and he'd reconsidered Jilly, embracing her slight weight, how it seemed odd but not unwelcome, like the moon out on a hot morning.

Now he looked at the moon and at the fine hairs on Kylie's arm.

How much of Kylie could he hope to retain beyond what was comforting, familiar? Her body against his was a temporary shield. He would have to let her go.

"William?" Janis was at his door. "Get up."

He rolled over. The red glow of his alarm clock sharpened into focus — 6:10 am. He rolled over, got up and climbed into his jeans, on the floor where they had been abandoned the evening before. Shirtless, he opened the door.

"Are you awake?" she asked. Janis had wound her hair up on top of her head and stabbed it into place with a set of chopsticks.

"Huh?"

"The crabapple blossoms. Today's the day. It's beautiful." Janis looked over her shoulder at the sky. "Delicious," she added.

"What? What for?"

"I invited you, didn't I? Last week when we were doing the crossword? Well, anyway, hurry." With that she went back upstairs.

William pulled on a T-shirt. In front of the mirror, he tried to straighten his bed head. It didn't work, so he splashed his face with cold water, drenched his long, dark hair and brushed his teeth. How did he look? Likely, he imagined, no better or worse than he was supposed to, especially this early.

"You realize this is my only morning to sleep in," he said as he entered her kitchen.

"Oh, you'll sleep later. Take this basket outside? Thanks sweetie." She did not look at him as she said this. She said it with her head in the freezer, she said *sweetie* to the frozen peas, to the ice cream, to the chicken fingers.

Janis spread two blankets out under the crabapple tree, now in full bloom. "It's my mock-Japanese party," she began. "Seventh year running. It started when I first moved in." Janis circled around William, who sat cross-legged in the centre of a blanket. "The first nice day, as soon as the blooms are out, I invite a friend over, and we have a picnic under the budding branches. It's a celebration of renewal." Janis reminisced about her friends — Maggie, Alice and Cynthia — and William deduced that he was the first man in seven years who'd been invited. "Seven years ago was when I left Robin, my ex-husband," she told him.

William, uncomfortable, uncrossed and then re-crossed his legs. He wondered why April, who was half Japanese, had never done anything like this.

Janis unpacked bread sticks, honey, apples, dates, brie, cranberries, raspberries, strawberries, pears, grapes and, most important, gin and tonic, ice wine, homemade cider, dandelion wine.

With spring coiling around them, they were drunk by the crack of dawn.

Under the yellow-blue sky, under red, red blossoms, falling droplets of dew and green sprouts, William lay down. Janis slid an ice cube made of gin and something into his mouth. He lowered his head onto her lap. Bird songs. Honey on his tongue from her finger, her light blue eyes, gold tumblers. Above them crimson spirals floating in blue.

Alone.

She pulled the blanket out from under him, damp with blades of new grass clinging to it. William lay still as she slid next to him. For a stray moment, he became clear-headed about what was happening, he felt her move in small progressions. They were hidden by the blanket, the new foliage, the shadow of the house next door. Her breath against his cheek. He closed his eyes. Everything felt cold. Her mouth, now almost against his, their downcast eyes, gin lips. A pause, long enough to raise the temperature, long enough for a second thought.

Given the oppressive Australian heat and the dense Sydney traffic, the drive from the eastern suburbs was painful and slow. *All this way*, Curt thought, *to collect two boxes I can't even remember packing.*

"It's your handwriting on the lids," his father assured him. "Time to take responsibility for what's yours, mate."

When he stood over the boxes in the garage, looking at the familiar letters — a mixture of lower and upper case — he had to admit, it *was* his boyish handwriting. He carried the boxes out of the garage and back up the driveway to his car, lowering them into the boot. The sun beat down. Salty beads of perspiration ran into his eyes and mouth.

Curt wandered through the house and out onto the verandah, looking for his father so he might say hello and goodbye. The backyard lay below him. It was a short strip of turf he had worshipped as a child. He played cricket there for whole days at a time as a young boy, turning the trampoline on its side to act as the wicket keeper so he wouldn't hit the house and break windows.

Mostly he'd imitate great Australian fast bowlers such as Dennis Lillie. Preparation for the first delivery was broadcast over imaginary loudspeakers: *"It's a balmy day here at the Sydney Cricket Ground, not too hot, slight southerly breeze. Great day for cricket. And, so, to start things off, it's the world's leading wicket taker, from his long run, that begins only just inside the long-*

off boundary." Curt had begun to jog on the spot. A fast bowler such as Lillie had a long run that might have been forty paces, but here, bowling on a very short pitch into a trampoline tipped on its side, there was just enough room for four symbolic paces. Curt would mark time for the first thirty-six mimicking his hero's perfect strides, side-on delivery, running his fingers over the ball pretending to bowl his leg cutters and as the corker thumped into the trampoline and popped right back out, he'd dive and take a classic catch.

From the verandah, Curt took one last look at the backyard, holding it still for a moment in his mind's eye. *Suddenly the fans in the members' stand were on their feet. The Englishman, Ian Botham, was at the crease with his easy stance, a string of six slips readied themselves on their toes, the long off, cover and extra cover charged in with the bowler, Dennis Keith Lillie himself this time, a leg cutter, an edge, the outstretched red glove of Marsh, and all fifty-five thousand Sydneysiders in the crowd along with fifteen million other Australians across the country screamed "He's got him" and "How is that one!" And there's Thomo and Border and Doug Walters, all with Lillie — long red stripes down his legs, baggy green caps on their heads and white zinc-creamed noses. The nation took a long gulp of cold beer and sang "C'mon Aussi, C'mon" while strangers and mates became one and the poor pom made his way back to the pavilion, followed by a cartoon golden duck.*

In the house Curt found his old man packing in the master bedroom.

"So, you're off? I'll see you next weekend in the city, eh mate?"

"Yeah, reckon so. Think you'll be unpacked?"

"Oh yeah. She's a pretty organized woman, Debbie is."

"I'll miss you at the funeral, though."

His father continued to mummify the mirror he was wrapping, the tape screeching as he tore it from the roll with his teeth. With a large black pen, he scrawled "bedroom contents."

"As I said, mate … Listen, sure you don't wanna come to my farewell barby?"

"I've really got to get home."

Before returning to the eastern suburbs, Curt drove to his old public school. He walked through the gate and across the black asphalt. When he was first a pupil here, the school was full to bursting. They'd had semi-portable classrooms, weather sheds, separate toilet blocks and new monkey bars. But by 1980 they were short on children; Friday-afternoon cricket was being *abolished*. Funding had been cut.

Now a beach suburb that had evolved into a destination of choice for retirees threatened to swallow the playground that spread out around him like a vacant lot. The portables, weather sheds, monkey bars and young families were all gone. Only the main school building still stood. Its proud black lettering confirmed its age: *c. 1924.*

Curt stumbled across a heel-gnawed brass plaque that lay in a square of sunken cement at the foot of the school's flagpole.

This time capsule, sealed in 1974, commemorates
the 50th anniversary of this school. It is to be
opened on the centennial anniversary, in 2024.

Curt looked back across the empty asphalt. Seagulls swooped and soared into the dazzling white sun.

In 1974 he was seven years old.

We won the war, in 1974, we kicked the bastards out the door in 1974. Arm in arm, the seven boys continued to chant, this time louder: *We won the war, in 1974 …*

During the morning assembly, Mr. Henty had reminded them, "Please play footy on the grass, not on the asphalt."

… we kicked the bastards out the door in 1974.

"Hey you blokes. Can I play?"

The seven boys stopped chanting and, without breaking the linked chorus line, turned to see who it was.

"Oh, Curtis, ya wog. Get fucked." Slacko, a foot taller than everyone else, gave the orders.

"Yeah, get fucked," Steve-o, the smallest boy piped in.

"We can use my new footy," said Curt.

The other six boys looked at Slacko.

"Give us a look," said Slacko.

Curt threw the ball to him. Slacko couldn't free his arms from the two boys at his sides in time to catch it properly. Slacko fell in love with the shiny pigskin with tight lacing and "Official Rugby League Ball" painted on the side in black and blue.

"Ahhh … run! Curtis is a greasy wog." With the ball wedged under one arm Slacko took off with his gang in tow.

Curt sank his hands in his pockets and walked over to a tree. There he slumped under the shade and dug a hole with a stick in the sandy soil, letting the dirt trickle through his fingers. He caught a horsefly that landed on his leg, removed its wings and dropped it into the hole. It tried to crawl up the sides. Before lunch ended Curt had seven wingless flies in the hole between his legs.

All these years later, the school still had big gum trees whose roots, like children's fingers working Plasticine, ran along, beneath and through the hot asphalt quad that had softened and given under the heat of two thousand days of Australian sun. Curt stood in the trees' shade now, in the very spot where he'd narrowly escaped his first kiss. They had chanted "Do it! Do it!" before he'd taken off to the squawking cries of "Chicken!" Sally Hopkins hadn't moved a muscle. Her eyes had remained wide, frozen.

In the distance white foam trailed the old ferry leaving the wharf. It was heading toward a tiny suburb nestled in the yellow sandstone cliffs and bush. Across the bay the gum trees threw familiar bits of silver light onto the water and down by the cricket oval an old woman tossed bread to the swooping seagulls. Farther down the bay gold and green spinnakers were flying high, and over by the marina roamed two red setters. It was an isolated place, unaware of its own isolation.

His old man was moving into a unit on the North Shore. Why come down here ever again, this spit of land cut off from Sydney, from the rest of the world by train tracks, inlets, rivers, sea and bush? Home seemed elsewhere. The pair of red setters came into view again, and he watched them for a time, before staring off at the flat horizon. Down here the Pacific Ocean falls away to the edge of the Earth. Loss, such gorgeous loss.

The summer after his first year of art college, when William was twenty and penniless, his father convinced him to move home. *You can use the basement for a studio.* He could help out around the house for pocket money. It was a time of savage disappointment.

The oil paints he was trying to master were useless. He spoiled canvases, wasted money, missed downtown, yearned for college to begin again. He felt degraded, sleeping alone in his boyhood bed, the bottom sheet still Darth-fucking-Vader. Nightly he longed for escape.

Those solitary summer months spent trapped in his parent's basement drove him to paint huge, nude, apolitical figures in a mock-rococo style by day and by night to comb through his adolescence, going over the clandestine afternoons he'd spent with his high school girlfriend, Elizabeth Kent. He'd stepped over awkward terrain: Elizabeth had taken pity on a brown-skinned boy. Her affection, her popularity, was all that had saved him. She had whitened his skin.

Sitting for days on the red couch, the summer heat mixing in the unair-conditioned basement with stifling paint fumes, William knew his life was like the horizon — everything lay on the opposite shore. If only he could see far enough to paint it.

Tonight, as he walked the boardwalk along Lake Ontario, the moon lit the purple night sky. His family's house — its two storeys, forest-green garage door, brass numbers, basketball hoop, silver Pontiac in the driveway — was a world away. Home was now the bustle of Chinatown or Little Italy, Toronto.

William watched a pair of red setters chase each other through the lakeside park, in and out through pockets of darkness. He stood on the grass overlooking the black lake, the emptiness of it, lights flickering on sailboat masts, the odd seagull landing to inspect a washed-up carp.

Suddenly he hated his parents. He simply had to get out, to forget, suppress, destroy his suburban, ordinary, forgettable self. He raged. He would forget everything, start again. He was an artist. He was adopted. He owed them nothing. Nothing.

All Curt remembered was a group of boys busting into the shower room, Slacko in the lead. Someone threw a towel over his head. He hit the tiled floor with his elbow, kneecap, hip, face. Strong hands parted his cheeks, and he felt finger after finger shoved into his anus and his own shit smeared all over his body, in his dark hair, his ear. He bit his bottom lip.

"You're not the captain. Get fucked, ya fuckin' wog," said Slacko. His voice was hateful. He booted Curt in the stomach.

Curt stood alone under the cold shower. His elbow hurt, his left knee throbbed, his nose was bleeding and the soap dispenser was empty.

The next year Curt's mother moved to the city.

JONATHAN BENNETT

William didn't see the punch coming. Trent Olds, the new kid at school, was good at everything. He played hockey in a Toronto league, he had a black jacket with red leather arms — *The Devils* the crest said — to prove it. His hair was long. But William was taller than Trent, and when Trent pushed in front of him in the batting line-up at softball practice William didn't think anything of it. Next thing William heard was "Fuckin' wop," and he was on the ground, warm, sweet blood pouring from his nose, running down the back of his throat. "A baseball hit him, Miss. I don't know where it came from," Trent said through the haze of William's pain.

William let the lie stand, never confronted Trent about it. His nose was broken and he told his father it "hurt like heck" when he arrived direct from work to collect William from the school infirmary. "Careful," his dad said. "Watch that language."

William had blood all down his T-shirt. The ice pack against his face gave him a headache that reached deep into his skull.

Unchecked nostalgia drew Curt to his father's farewell barbecue even though he'd declined the invitation. He wanted to
say goodbye to this place, to his home, to old family friends.

It was at his uncle's place, overlooking the bay, built into a
cliff only a few degrees shy of sheer. Several hundred steps
ran along the side of the house and down to the waterfront.
The gate clanked shut, and all eyes turned as Curt descended
the stairs. He saw the familiar group: Uncle Bill, Ray, Avril,
Stephen, Claudia, Nadine, Josh and Faye, Dr. Jenkins, half a
dozen neighbours he'd seen many times before but couldn't
always name and a few stray kids. They mulled around,
drinking beer, eating potato salad, steak and sausage sandwiches off paper plates.

"Curt, mate, how's it garn?"

"G'day, your old man's over there strappin' the feed bag
on."

"Curt, ya poor prick, getta beer, ya boof head."

"What's the score, Curt? Did ya drive, mate?"

"Hello, Curtis. Did you get something to eat, darling?"

As he wandered through the gathering, the guests smiled,
nodded and cajoled. They were like his father — men and
women who started with nothing, worked hard and raised
kids. Their skin was leathery, their eyeballs bloodshot, their
noses bloated and their voices loud. They made deep-rooted

accusations in lighthearted ways. As always, they were right-eous and loyal, intelligent and unreasonable.

Curt stayed for less than an hour. Halfway up the stairs, it occurred to him that his mother had once known these people too, yet not one of them had mentioned her name. No one had said, "I'm sorry to hear about Margaret" or "How are you coping, Curt?"

The sun shimmered off the road in a mirage of heat and exhaust. Botany Bay opened up to his right as he considered the two planes that circled overhead, waiting to land, the run-way stretching out into the water. We're all bound to Botany Bay — dreaming our departures, corroborating our arrivals.

When William awoke it was five in the afternoon. He rolled over, his futon creaking, and in a flash he recalled the blossoms, raspberries, gin, Janis' light blue eyes. His phone was ringing.

April. Her characteristically frugal choice of words gave shape to short, even thoughts. It was irritating. William felt the first twang of a headache, but he tried to concentrate. *Could he come and collect the paintbrushes he loaned her last year? Did he want to sign a separation agreement? For mutual protection. It was up to him, she didn't mind either way*, and then the pause before she hung up. *Take care.*

The sky darkened as clouds passed over the low-lying sun. William closed his eyes. He could still hear April's mollifying voice. He pulled up the covers, closing his hand around himself. He groaned and rolled onto his back, his hands gripping his throbbing head. He stayed perfectly still for a moment, and the pounding passed. His mind relaxed, fell away, in and out of sleep.

And then, for the first time in several years, without any warning, he dreamed of his brother. The dream woke him up. His twin was the one secret he had kept from April. He hadn't told her early enough in the relationship, and then it became too big a secret to have kept at all.

Secrets. His. Mine. *Us*, he sighed to himself. He could hear Janis' footsteps walking across the floor above him, the odd mumbled word. Janis was pacing, talking on the phone per-haps. William drifted off to sleep.

William first saw April Tanaka during his first week of art college. She tossed her long hair, sat in the front row, wore a rust-coloured, second-hand suede jacket, had light brown skin.

At first he hated her art.

By the second year, her work's purpose had become to "mar Western capitalist icons." With a stiff face and a clenched left fist, April educated the women in their class. She had a T-shirt made that said *Stab Back with Your Brush*. April was furious.

He watched her from the back row.

She dated one guy after the next: Juan, Colin, Juan again, Mustafa.

They'd spoken only seven times in three and a half years. Finally she said, *Why don't you just paint through your culture?*

William shrugged.

By Christmas break they were the talk of the class. They moved in together within weeks, painted in tandem, showed their work in an empty mall store. April asked William relent-less questions about his past: *Why is your skin brown? Where are your birth parents? What nationality are you?* She told him about her uncle's incestuous advances, how she ran away at sixteen. William fell in love with her to save her. They fought and made up weekly. It lasted five years. Five years of growth, back-burning and regrowth.

The mourners ushered themselves past Curt and left the church in single file. Outside they swarmed on the grass beside the flowers. Around the church the reverend's wife had planted hibiscuses, their deep red petals splayed to reveal yellow stamens. Only the minister remained inside the church with Curt, fussing over a few hymn books that had fallen off the front pew. He glanced over at Curt more than once.

Curt remained still, head in his hands, concentrating on his mother's note, her words, face, fingers. When he was young, she used to pat his cheek, stroke his dark hair. She used to make his lunch, to "make him grow up strong." After the divorce, she became a confidante, a collaborator, an ally.

She'd hated herself.

Through his tears he saw the stained-glass panes behind the altar. Shards of primary colour fell in and out of focus.

The reverend gave up the pretence of tidying the fallen hymn books. His steps echoed as he crossed the marble aisle. Curt was alone.

Aunt Jilly, who wore an inappropriate dress to the funeral (bright green with rows of purple flowers) cried in fits and shudders during the first half of the service. When it was her turn to speak, she sobbed her way through a homily about living life to the fullest before collapsing back into her pew. It was only a fraction of what she'd told Curt she was going to say.

He ran the service over and over in his mind. His mother

had not asked for a specific type of funeral in her will. He stared at the empty space where her casket had been only minutes before, and suddenly he felt that he should have gone up to speak.

After the inadequate eulogy, Aunt Jilly's eyes roamed the faces of the mourners for a sympathetic nod, for forgiveness. Curt complied. It released itself, an involuntary reflex action — a half smile that emanated more from his eyes than his mouth.

"Curt? Are you still in here?" Kylie had been outside shaking hands, squeezing forearms in a manner that implied more sympathy and pain than were true or required on her part. She'd felt self-conscious. "Curt. You should come outside. People need to talk with you."

As they walked down the aisle and out of the church, Kylie took Curt by the hand.

"Do you know what I've just realized?" he said.

"What?"

"I don't have any memories from before I was about six years old. That's late, don't you think?"

Outside the day filled with light and the smell of hibiscus and gum trees. Women in black dresses, sunglasses and wide-brimmed hats stood in tight circles, grieving, mourning, perspiring. The men leaned against nearby trees, doing the right thing by their wives simply by being there. The women were fellow teachers from the school where Margaret had worked for years, old girlfriends from teachers college or high school.

Curt approached Jilly first. She reached out and touched his cheek, attempted to smile. Kylie led Curt in a wide weave through the crowd; people nodded at him. There were only a few tears.

"William," Francisco began, "be a good lad and stack those," he said, pointing to the silk screens that covered the entire back work table. They were both tired, this job had taken them far longer than they'd anticipated. "Today ugly prints for rich people, and tomorrow ..." here he paused and theatrically threw his hands on his hips "... Italian sunshine, art and cappuccino." They both laughed.

It was late, close to ten. Philip had worked the entire day up front, in the showroom, doing the cash and taking orders while William and Francisco painted, waltzed, framed, sang, drew, mimed, glued. Philip had left the shop earlier to go home and pack. He and Francisco were off to the Italian Riviera for their annual vacation.

"What are *you* going to do for the next two weeks?" Francisco asked William almost as an afterthought as he collected the screens.

Francisco was from Manchester originally and still had remnants of an accent. He was short and had a round, red face. He taught art and design part time at the college. William had been his favourite student, so Francisco had persuaded Philip to give him a summer job at the store — based on his first exhibition. Summer turned into part-time and then full-time work.

Even though they most often worked on interior, decorative, made-to-order jobs, William knew he would learn from

Francisco every day. This had been their relationship for some years now.

"What am I going to do?" William ran a screen under the tap, massaging it with his fingers to remove the paint. "Not sure. Probably just spend some time with Janis."

"We're going to have to meet this Janis person on our return, see if Philip and I approve of her. Really, then, how old *is* she?"

The next morning William drove Philip and Francisco to the airport. After they disappeared behind the check-in counters, William looked around the huge steel concourse of Terminal 3 at Toronto International Airport: its marbleized floors, stark white girders and multilingual Coke advertisements. He watched the people coming and going for a moment, duty-free shopping bags, suitcases, the beginnings of jet lag and airplane constipation slowing them down.

As William drove Philip's fifteen-year-old grey Saab through the streets of Toronto, contemplated the day. It was nine in the morning. It was a Saturday in late May, with the new greens and the fragile heat of an early summer in the air. He knocked on Janis' door.

"I can't, William. I have to finish editing this," Janis said, sitting cross-legged in the middle of the floor in an oversized white T-shirt.

"Oh, come on, it's a perfect day for Toronto Island. A *delicious* spring day," he said.

She smiled. "William, I'm busy. This is written by a friend of mine. I'm returning a favour."

"Finish it later." He squatted down next to her, pages covered in red pen marks and yellow flags spread out around her splayed legs. "C'mon," said William in a last-ditch effort. "I've got a car. We'll take the ferry, have a picnic."

William watched the thick ropes loop around the solid metal spools on the wharf, listened as the old ferry moaned, rubbing against the thick slabs of rubber and old tires on the wooden pilings. Seagulls squawked, children squealed, a radio played an old 70s song, he smelled his first barbecue of the season.

He and Janis wandered down the boardwalk on the far side of the island: rollerbladers, bikers, families playing Frisbee.

"Who's your friend?" asked William.

"Which friend?"

"The friend who wrote the manuscript you're working on."

"Oh, just a guy I've known for years." She laughed a little, her eyes a deeper blue, reflecting the water. She paused. "William, why would you want to spend a day like today with me?"

He considered her question and shrugged his shoulders. A seagull took to the air to avoid a small boy on a bike. He thought of April.

"I had a twin brother once," he said, surprising himself.

"What do you mean?" Janis stopped walking and faced him.

"I was adopted. I was four or so, but somewhere I have an identical twin brother." William looked out over the lake.

"Your brother ... did your parents tell you? Do you remember him?"

"They didn't tell me, they might not even realize I know ... but I remember him."

They walked on until they found a good spot. Janis unpacked a knapsack: a blanket, cheddar cheese, French bread, a bottle of mineral water and a thermos full of gin, vermouth, ice and lemonade.

"I also remember my father, my real father. He had darker skin than I do. I remember a park. I can't remember my mother. I've tried. Those images in my memory are like bad photographs, grainy and distant."

"A twin brother. That's incredible. Have you ever tried to contact him? Or any of them?"

"No. You met my mother when I moved in; she's pretty fragile."

"So you've never tried?"

"My dad asked me a long ago not to talk about being adopted; it upsets my mom, though sometimes *she* brings it up."

"Do you think about it a lot?"

"No. No, not really." William poured them each a drink from the thermos. As they ate, the sun warmed the air.

"We haven't ever talked about what happened under the crabapple tree that day," said Janis, rifling through the knapsack for a chocolate bar.

"What's to say?" he said, closing his eyes as he faced the sun.

"What are you so smug about?" she said, annoyed.

Was she angry at the truant chocolate bar, at exposing her feelings, at the vermouth that no doubt played a part in her finding the courage to bring it up? William reached over and kissed her neck, gently.

"William," her voice hovered, "how old are you?"

"Twenty-seven. You?"

"Just turned thirty-nine," she said, breathing in, his lips again close.

He slid his hand across her neck, behind her thick brown-grey hair, thinking only for a moment of April. Janis tilted her head up toward him.

In the background Lake Ontario remained quiet, barely licking the warming rocks that lined the shore. Spring slid into summer that quiet afternoon, in full view of the city.

After the service most of the mourners returned to Jilly's house. Curt spent much of the afternoon on the back verandah with Kylie looking at his old high school. When his parents divorced, everyone knew it was because of her drinking, her mood swings, her depression. She'd been difficult for so long that Curt's father eventually tossed her out. At least that is how Curt understood it.

He must have known something of his mother's unhappiness growing up, at least sensed it. Margaret didn't leave the flat much except to go to work, to the shops. She never saw other men, at least as far as he could tell. But lately her mood had been better, that was what was most confusing. She'd begun playing tennis with Jilly and last Christmas she went on a holiday up to the Gold Coast.

Admittedly she came back and pretended nothing had happened, that she'd never gone. "Lovely" was all she'd say to his questions. "It was lovely." Instead she refocused on *his* life, as she'd done for years, prodding him for information about Kylie, his friends, his plans. But even so she *had* gone away. He thought she'd been making an effort.

When Curt moved out of the flat and in with Kylie, his mother began to drink more heavily. Her doctor put her on medication to help her cope with her loneliness.

Curt visited her almost daily, and many evenings he and Kylie would go over for dinner. On the worst days, when

Margaret hadn't made it to work or even gotten out of bed, they'd do the cooking. The three of them stuck it out for several months and Margaret improved. Life, for a time, seemed to find a new rhythm.

"I can't believe your father didn't come," said Kylie.

Curt wondered if his father had it in him to console. Perhaps he should start something new between them. Maybe he'd better try.

Across the field the school building with its huge clock face and tower loomed above them. As a sixteen year old sitting on the grassy hill at school he'd felt as if everything around him — the buildings, his mates, his mother, his father — towered over him, as if he could not control even this little corner of his life.

"It's not Dad's fault," Curt said quietly. "My mother's friends hate him now."

Kylie put her hand on his leg. Patted it twice.

"When I was playing my first cricket game there, I got hit on the back of the head with the ball and got a goose egg. I wouldn't take my cricket cap off, I was so embarrassed." They laughed a little as the sun dipped behind a cloud and the bells in the clock tower rang to announce three o'clock.

Janis took William to her favourite Vietnamese restaurant in Chinatown, where they chose a booth under a green dragon mural toward the rear of the restaurant.

He presented his theories on his genealogy. "For a while I thought I was Native, you know, Indian, because I saw a photograph of a Cree man who looked quite like me. Then I thought I was Maltese. Then Armenian. Then April decided I was more likely half something."

"Who's April?" asked Janis.

"My ex. She is half Japanese. But let's not talk about her."

"Okay, so half something."

"Right. So then I thought I might be half Italian, half Pacific islander, you know, like a Maori from New Zealand, or a Tongan, or an Australian Aborigine because of my skin colour and nose. But now I think I may be something else because I met an anthropologist on New Year's Eve who guessed I am half Malaysian, or Thai, or Filipino and perhaps something European. Maybe I'm even part Turkish, or Jewish, or Mexican." He paused. "So that's what I know."

"Good God."

Janis insisted on paying for everything and they walked home holding hands. It was a warm Toronto night, July 1st, Canada

Day. With the sweet, naked taste of summer in their mouths, they climbed the stairs to Janis' bedroom.

The dark corners of the room fell away into depthlessness, black water. The room was a circle, an oval, hollow, surrounded in soft orange light and through the open window the remnants of the day dissolved beneath a weak moon.

Janis — like women he admired on the subway, women who until now had undressed themselves outside his comprehension — arched and fell with his movements.

He memorized her: like a draftsman, he considered the arch of her foot, her toes, from beneath, peas in a half pod, the fine veins zigzagging up her leg. There was much of her he wanted to draw.

Curt sat on a stool in his father's new kitchen looking at the photographs of Debbie and his father, one on each side of a silver hinged frame. His father as a young man, with thick, sun-blond Australian hair, curly about his ears, as he smiled, squinting in the camera. In the twin frame opposite was an older studio portrait of Debbie. She sat with her hands crossed on her lap and her head cocked slightly up and to the left. The burgundy background accented her mustard shirt and her earrings were gold, large and now out of fashion.

Curt looked from one half of the dual frame to the other. His father was partially cast in shadow. A crisp outline of a face ran down his cheek ... his mother's shadow. *Had either of them seen this?* Curt wondered. *Would they have considered cutting into my father's face to remove it?* Curt imagined his shadowless, severed mother in a shoe box somewhere with miscellaneous negatives of himself as a toddler and old Kodachrome slides of his parents' honeymoon. Debbie, on the other hand, had never been married, so the expression Curt read on her face was more like a plea: *When, when will I find love?*

Curt looked around. His father had been right, Debbie *was* organized. In less than a week their new place was in remarkable order. Not only were the pictures hanging in symmetrical clusters, but the furniture was arranged, she'd folded and

stacked the linen in the closet, matched the towels in the bathroom and thoughtfully angled the rugs in the living room.
Debbie displayed a sensitivity to the natural flow of house-
hold foot traffic, even though it would be light.

"Curt, I'm off to the grog shop. Coming?" asked his father.

"No. I'll stay."

"Don't move anything, then."

I have no place here, Curt thought. Earlier he'd had to ask his
father for a beer. It was not his house, not his fridge. These
were things belonging to two other people, people he half
knew. There was almost no evidence of his childhood, that it
had ever existed.

He was yesterday, accommodated by a restless today and
resented by an impending tomorrow. He would not discuss
his mother's death with his father. It would be an exercise in
humiliation for them both. Their relationship was over; the
adoption had expired.

Curt stepped outside onto the balcony. Their place looked
out over Sydney harbour from a great height. The inlets
twisted, grabbing wavefuls of earth to return to the sea. The
terracotta roofs of the waterfront suburbs stepped down to the
harbour's edge between bursts of trees, swimming pools and
glimpses of bitumen.

Both Curt and his father were Sydneysiders, men who
looked into the sun, could navigate coastal roads, gnarled suburbs, train lines, rivers and bays. And their mouths could say
the names along the way: Narrabeen, Woollahra, and
Cronulla, Parramatta and Katoomba. The hard land at their
backs, the ocean and the horizon before them.

A cloud passed overhead and briefly cast Curt in shadow.
In these moments he had allowed a single treasonous thought

to take hold: *He would leave Sydney.* Perhaps he'd polluted the place where he'd grown up so that there was nothing left. His job at the music store was a dead end. Everything with Kylie had collapsed. Things had become unhinged long before his mother died.

Yet, although the band was going nowhere, he was writing music faster than ever. From the moment he'd read his mother's letter, her oddly shaped *M*, he'd felt the music inside him, note after note, issuing from his hands.

He would go to Spain, to France, to England. He would use his small inheritance. He needed to get out and this time his mother could not guilt him into staying.

"St. Francis of Assisi," Francisco began, "whose real name was Giovanni di Bernardone, was born in 1182 and died in 1226. He was an Italian friar born, as the name suggests, in Assisi. More wine, Janis? William? Philip?"

"Why do you always stand up when you tell this story?" said Philip, casting Janis an apologetic look.

"It's not a story. It's history," Francisco said. "As I was saying, St. Francis of Assisi renounced worldly goods in 1205 to live in poverty and devote himself to prayer. He founded the Franciscans in 1209 and was made a saint in 1228. This year, when we visited Italy, Philip and I saw a magnificent painting of St. Francis of Assisi. He was sitting in the country-side among animals and birds. Every year I have a party on October 4th, his feast day."

"He invites his friends over and they drink and tell ribald stories," said Philip. "What that's got to do with piety and the Catholic church I'll never know."

"No," said Francisco, "I don't suppose you will, Philip of Boringshire."

"I have a celebration every year," interrupted Janis, looking to William for help.

"Yes," began William, "every year, on the first nice week-end in spring, Janis wakes up one of her friends at the crack of dawn and has him or her join her in her backyard so they can get blind drunk before the sun comes up."

"Bravo," said Francisco, clapping his hands. "I approve of this one."

"There's more to it than that," said Janis. "I have a flowering crabapple tree in my backyard. When it first blooms, the blossoms are so delicious they beg for a celebration. So this year I invited William, who I *thought* had a good time."

"Oh, I *did*," said William.

"Is Francis your patron saint?" asked Janis.

"Well," said Francisco, "I try to practise the same conscientiousness in my art that he did in his religious life. But I'm not very pious and haven't taken vows of poverty, couldn't even think of taking a vow of chastity."

Philip threw up his arms. He was laughing, taking the performance in stride. "If we let Francisco completely take over this conversation, he'll point it downhill," said Philip, "and I know from experience that the slope is a slippery one. Francisco, why don't you help me with the dishes?"

While Philip and Francisco walked back and forth from the kitchen to the dining room carrying dirty dishes and cutlery, Fritz, their dog, circled the table hoping for leftovers. William and Janis took a seat on the couch in the front room.

"I feel like I'm meeting your parents," said Janis now that they were alone.

"Well, you and I at a dinner party at Ruth and Roger's in suburbia ... that'll never happen, so this is as close as you'll get."

"Great house. They've done so much with it. I used to have a place like it with Robin. Two storeys. I was there for twelve years. We bought it with Robin's inheritance right after we were married. After the money was divided between him and his three brothers, he had just enough to make a downpayment and open his bookstore."

Francisco and Philip returned with glasses of port and conversation continued well into the night. With the front windows wide open, the sounds of cafés and restaurant patios, the roar of muscle cars, dogs barking and streetcars screeching floated into the room.

"We'd better go," said Janis at midnight.

In the taxi on the way home, her leg shifted against his and her hand moved to his thigh. Outside: the night, the street-lights, sounds of the city. The taxi driver's sitar music plucked quietly.

"I don't want this to become an everyday thing," she began, "but will you stay with me tonight?"

"I'll bet you didn't know that your mother introduced me to my wife."

Curt focused on the one grey hair stranded on top of Jeffrey Bates' head. As his mother's longtime solicitor, Jeffrey was prone to reminiscing.

"We were at a B&S together in Dubbo and your mother dragged me over to meet Carol, who was …"

As Jeffrey talked, Curt drifted to the melody in his head. He thought that if he got up to leave he might lose it, so he sat still, letting the notes replay themselves in his mind over and over again. In the end Jeffrey suggested that Curt cash a bond to finance his trip.

With letters, deeds and certificates transferring his mother's estate to his own, Curt walked down New South Head Road to the bank. Since he'd be travelling, he named Jeffrey as interim caretaker.

"No, nothing. Sorry." The travel agent's nails tapped the keyboard while her eyes remained fixed on the computer screen. "You could go the other way, if you really can't wait until next week. I could put you on a flight that goes via Honolulu to Toronto and from there you can connect to Madrid."

"Great. As long as I can leave tomorrow," said Curt.

"You'll have a layover in Toronto while you wait for the connecting flight to Madrid."

"Perfect."

JONATHAN BENNETT

The dust hung heavily in the dull light as William wandered
toward the back of the bookstore. He sized up Robin behind the
counter, reclining in his chair, talking on the phone to a difficult
customer. He had a coarse black-and-grey beard, bifocals, and
he was thin, stringy even. He wore a pair of new-looking jeans,
a white dress shirt beneath a brown suede vest and silver jewellery. He was perhaps fifty.

William had had a couple of beers with lunch and now the
books swarmed around him. As did the neat calligraphic sec-
tion signs: MILITARIA, BOTANICA, OCEANIA, MODERN FIRSTS.
Finally he found ART. He looked for a book he could afford,
something to engage Robin in conversation. Something to find
out what he was up against. Janis had said, after all, that she
hadn't spoken with him in four years. She'd moved on, made
new friends, grown.

Robin was trying to convince the phone customer that it
was not a first edition he owned but a reprint. "No, it's worth-
less. Get a second opinion, then … ," he was saying. He spoke
with confidence and precision. "I don't want to oversimplify,
but selling used books is raw capitalism. I'm the buyer, you're
the seller. You don't have the right goods. I'm not buying. It's
not personal." His voice was level, confident and remarkably
free of sarcasm. It was the voice of a man comfortable being an
expert. He was commanding. He ended the conversation only
to make another call.

William found a copy of Cellini's autobiography, illustrated by Salvador Dalí, and he walked confidently to the front desk, turning the book's spine down in his hot palm. Robin remained on the phone. He hardly looked up, only raising an eyebrow to acknowledge William's presence. He made change with the phone wedged under his chin, then slipped the book into a brown paper bag and slid it across the counter. Still on the phone, he plucked a large reference book from the shelf behind him. *Asshole.*

Instead of returning directly home, William walked west along a tree-lined street. It was one of the many he walked down months ago when he was looking for an apartment. It had been grey and dull then: dirty snow piled up along the gutters, the bare trees surrounded by brown tufts of grass floating, on frozen and muddy lawns. Now the oak and maple trees shone in the sun. The light flickered across the bricks of old Victorian houses with heavy wooden doors and Art Nouveau flourishes. A dog accompanied a woman carrying her groceries.

William walked until he approached a large white house with an arched, stained-glass window. Number 24. Janis had talked of her old house fondly and, he now realized, faithfully. William felt a sudden urge to see *inside* it, to see why she left.

He reached for the latch, easing it up slowly and swinging the cast-iron gate open. He ducked alongside the house, crouching to see through a basement window, but at such an odd angle all he could see was carpet. He spent several minutes in this position, still clutching his Cellini, beginning to feel a little foolish. As he stood to leave, his eye caught the glint of something brass.

The spare key lay tucked underneath a large stone and

without too much trouble it fit the keyhole in the front door. As he crossed the threshold into the foyer, he slid the key into the pocket of his jeans.

Leather-bound books lined the walls of the living room: encyclopedia sets, art books, dictionaries, the complete works of Sir Walter Scott, Shakespeare, Dickens, botanical texts, Greek poetry and military history.

William wandered into the back room, which he supposed was Robin's office. His computer shared the desk with an old Smith Corona typewriter. An antique globe sat on the top of his wooden filing cabinet. A sprawling lithograph of a great battle hung on the wall above his desk. He stared at the tortured faces of the vanquished, impaled horses and the triumphant poses of the victors, their swords thrust into the sky, pointing toward God. He admired the detail of the old gilt frame.

In the kitchen William inspected the fridge. Robin had very little food, but a fine supply of salad dressings and condiments. He couldn't resist taking a beer. As he took a mouthful, he noticed a picture of Robin and a woman on the fridge. The woman looked remarkably like Janis, similar age, height, but harsher features, a finer nose, a sharper chin. He put the picture in his shirt pocket.

He downed the rest of the beer and left it on a nook beside a vase on a small landing halfway up the staircase.

In the bedroom William found a bottle of gin beside the clock radio. An exercise bike was parked in the corner of the room with a wet towel hanging from it. The unmade bed was king-sized. Its blue sheets did not match the green-and-brown pillow cases. In the ensuite bathroom, Robin's shaving cream can had left a rust stain on the counter top. The medicine cabinet contained various pills, Aspirin, Band-Aids and an open box of condoms. Three left.

Then, acting completely out of character, William did the most extraordinary thing: he took a shit in Robin's toilet, and, just as he was almost finished, just as he was reaching for the toilet paper, just as he had almost gotten away with it, William heard the front door open.

"Honey? Robin?" A woman's voice.

William gave himself a swift wipe and gathered his pants, pulling them up as he stood. He could hear the woman in the kitchen. He was having trouble with his belt — *Think quickly. Where to go? Where to go?* He considered the shower stall, but Robin's curtain was transparent. He crept across the bedroom, the floorboards giving an almighty creak.

William could hear the woman climbing the stairs. She must have stopped on the landing, perhaps picking up his beer bottle, because it took her a minute to get to the bedroom. By this time he had climbed into the large clothes closet, the door ajar only an inch.

Through the crack, William watched the woman, not ten feet away from him, light a cigarette and smoke it sitting on the bed. She tapped the ashes carefully into her hand. Then she walked into the bathroom.

"Oh, God, gross." The toilet flushed.

Now she was over by the exercise bike, near the window, and William could tell this woman was definitely not the woman in the photograph. She was much younger; she was his age. The front door opened again.

"Sylvia?" It was Robin.

"I'm up here."

William's heart was racing.

"Oh, look at *you*." Once again Robin's voice was precise, exacting.

It was now clear to William that although she was not in his line of sight, the woman, Sylvia, was at least partially undressed.

"Let me call Ann first," said Robin.

"Oh, don't bother," she pleaded.

"I have to. There's always a chance." Robin's voice thinned with impatience, but retained its command, cutting right to the quick. "Hi, Ann, it's me. Can you meet me for lunch in an hour? I'll close the store. We could go somewhere in Yorkville." There was a pause. "Right, no, I understand. I'll see you at home usual time, then." Another pause. "Me too. Bye."

Through the crack in the door, William realized he was about to witness a nooner, a clandestine lunch rendezvous. The whole thing took nine minutes. Robin spoke a lot, though not always about the matter at hand. Robin's penis was on the smallish side and took some attention on Sylvia's part to prepare for the task.

"Did you drink a beer?" Robin asked as he rotated Sylvia onto her stomach.

On the whole William considered the entire program a little passionless. Never having had an affair, he'd supposed them to be heady, wild, rampant. Were they not supposed to release pent-up frustrations gathered from unwanted, but as yet undiscarded, relationships? So what the hell was this lethargic poke? The whole thing reeked of the same force of habit it was meant to relieve.

They left together as quickly as they had arrived. William

waited inside the closet for another few minutes, to be sure. He remembered Janis' words: *He cheated on me for a year with a history professor, the bastard.*

William climbed out of the closet. He picked up the phone beside the bed and hit the redial button. A woman's voice answered.

"Ann?" His voice shook a little.

"Yes?"

"Robin's having an affair with a woman called Sylvia." William jammed his finger down on the receiver. His words had been clear and precise.

Serves you right.

He replaced the picture on the fridge and the key under the rock and left through the front gate.

Walking home, replaying the entire event in his mind, William realized he had left his Cellini in the closet. He considered going back to get it, but decided against it. Robin had hardly looked at him when he'd bought it. Besides, he probably wouldn't find it for a day or so and he'd have more important questions on his mind by then.

A white spotlight encircled Curt as he began his solo. The bassist quieted down. The drummer dusted the snare drum with brushes. Curt played soft, hesitant notes, asking the piano to guide him, lead him through a piece he'd played hundreds of times before. The old tuneless upright, stacked against the wall of the pub where his band played every Friday night, complied.

"C'mon," someone in the crowd urged.

Curt played more forcefully. His momentum grew. For the first time in more than a year, the song started to swing. This old jazz standard, this tune he'd rummaged around in, explored all the corners of many times before, finally gave up a new note. Then another.

Curt's mind drifted to his own compositions, their rhythms dark, modulating, in love with another place.

As the set ended to enthusiastic applause, Kylie entered wearing a long black dress. Her hair was up and her back straight. She'd often talked about how much she hated this pub, its sweaty musicians, and long ago she'd stopped coming to their Friday night gigs. Curt knew why she was here tonight.

"Do you want to tell me where you're going?" she said when she reached the stage.

Curt nodded in the direction of a table at the back of the pub and signalled to the bartender for two beers. "Europe. Spain first, then France, maybe England."

"When?" she asked.

"Tomorrow morning."

"Shit, Curt, that's …" Kylie paused for a moment, checking herself, "that's soon." She reached forward and took his hand in her own, stroked his upturned palm with her thumb. Her eyes were downcast. "When are you coming back?"

Curt withdrew his hand and lit a cigarette. "Not really sure. I'll write." Looking at her lips, mouth, he remembered her standing in the doorway of her bedroom only last week, naked, arms above her head, strong, lean.

She would meet him at the airport tomorrow morning. There would be no tears. He would go back to his mother's tonight. They both knew it was best.

Curt left, giving Kylie a kiss on the cheek, running his finger through her hair.

She sat and ordered bourbon-and-Cokes until she could no longer remember the look on his face when he left.

"I can't be very interesting," Janis said. She sat with her legs dangling from the kitchen counter, her hair up in chopsticks.

Across the room William made sweeping gestures with his arms as he scored the paper with hurried pencil lines. In his mind he blocked the page in thirds. He drew quickly, freely, sometimes only a few lines, barely giving her shape before tearing the sheet from his book.

"Are you hungry?" she asked, jumping down off the counter, signalling that the session was over.

Janis peeled and diced carrots. But he continued, drawing the curve under her arm leading up to her shoulder. New potatoes, washed, quartered. Her bottom, its join, its halves. Stock. Breast. Water. Hair. Salt. Lips. Celery. Leg. Pepper. Nose. Parsley.

After an hour William had thirty-six drawings, each with a different line, curves, a lightly shaded eye, a brow beside an ear, an arm here, a hip there. Meanwhile, Janis had made soup. He didn't show her the sketches.

Later, downstairs in his room, William added strokes of watercolour. He spread the drawings out across the floor and on several dripped, brushed, dashed a rusty red. Others he covered in denim blue. Some received forest green or a dull yellow. One that was more complete got a night-sky purple and he did several in a single swipe of watery black.

The next morning William took the sketches outside and photographed each one using Kodachrome colour-slide film. Under his feet the ground was damp. In the next few weeks, leaves would change colour and fall away.

Days later, piece by piece, line by line, William reassembled Janis. He had photographed each of the sketches intending to do some sort of collage, but when he saw the slides developed he put them in a projector to see what they looked like blown up. Each slide was from a different perspective. He traced each body part to a mounted sheet of paper on the wall. He could adjust the projected image for size. He put the projector on its side to do her leg. He drew her jawbone at a super-imposed forty-five-degree angle.

The next day at work he showed Francisco.

"Don't put your finger on the glass. Smudges. How did you do this?" asked Francisco.

"I cheated," said William. "I moved the original slide over the finished drawing until I found a swath of that colour. Sort of like a hand-held projector."

"Well, let's get it framed," said Francisco.

Francisco mounted the piece, put it on white card behind glass and finished it with a simple wooden frame.

"It's very sharp," Francisco said. He stopped for a moment and took the piece in. "Yes, it's excellent, William. Could you do another?"

"I'm not sure."

"Art should not be accidental. It's purposeful. You can't see it yet, but everything you're painting and creating right now … is about you. You don't want your art to have boundaries, borders. You can't take criticism because you don't know who you are."

"I drew *Janis*. She's not some pseudo-self-portrait," said William.

"Oh, yes she is," said Francisco, tearing a large piece of brown wrapping paper from the roll to wrap up the piece.

"Well, that's all beside the point. It's *her* impression that counts," said William. "I'm going to show her tonight."

Travelling along South Dowling Street in the cab on the way to the airport, Curt watched Sydney fly by in a blur. He wondered why there were so few people to say goodbye to.

As the open fields of Moore Park became grassy hills and golf courses, he considered his options. He could totally reinvent himself, his character traits, his history. He could be a stockman who broke wild brumbies; he could be the bloody "man from Snowy River" himself, for all anyone in Europe knew. He could be athletic. He could vote for the other side. He could certainly dress better. He could find God. He could become a vegetarian, a lawyer, an actor, an ophthalmologist, a surfer, a braggart, a misanthrope. If his mother could commit suicide, anything was possible.

The plane thundered along, bisecting the jagged international dateline. The air inside the cabin was thick and stale: coffee, beer, lavatory deodorizer, bodies. Reaching into his breast pocket, Curt withdrew his mother's letter. Then, from nothing, hot tears. She was gone. His eyes stung and his throat was raw and throbbing.

At the airport Curt had held Kylie close. He'd run his knuckles up and down her spine. He hadn't known at the time what this embrace meant, and he knew less about it now as he soared above the clouds. Kylie had pulled away from him and opened up his hand, placing in it something smooth, cool, metal. A gold lighter, engraved with the words *A Love Supreme.*

Curt thought about Kylie's reddened eyes, her thin lips, her hair lit by the sun, thought about how she'd nodded and walked away.

From his seat, through the double-paned porthole window, Curt stared at the flashing lights on the wing tip. Beyond them was darkness, atmosphere, pressure, nothing but the preconditions for next week's weather for a coastline of one country or another.

"Mum," he whispered to himself. A small voice. A lost sound. As if it were the first time he'd said it aloud since he was a boy. It meant something new up here. Someone new. Wherever she may be.

Noah's eyes climbed the dormant volcano in the distance. The park stretched out in front of him. Sunshine. Palm trees. Two young boys ran across the grass naked, their sleepy father chasing them, laughing, his arms outstretched. On a nearby blanket, the boys' mother turned the pages of a book. She looked up every few moments to watch. The boys looked like their father already, even though they were young, even though they were children.

Noah walked to this park almost every morning before starting work at the hotel. He walked along the same path, past the same stores with yellow-flowered dresses for sale and the currency exchange rates posted in the windows. The shop-keepers spoke English, Japanese, German and French — a few words of Latin if a sale depended on it.

Not far away the beach stretched out to water and sky. The ocean surrounded Noah like a moat. It reminded him that Hawaii was a long way away from his old habits, his old self. For more than twenty years he'd been clean, drug-free.

Noah watched the horizon for sea birds, the way they swooped and dove, taking to the air or to the sea. He couldn't help but wonder what it was like to soar as a bird did. He read a book on sea birds once. He couldn't remember the title if he was asked, but the book's sentiment has lurked in the back of his mind for years. Much like the smell of green tea wouldn't remind him precisely of his mother if he happened to smell it again, but it would almost definitely recall his childhood.

In the park Noah passed the old woman as he had every morning for ten years now. The old woman and Noah had never traded a word, but they acknowledged each other with a nod. The old woman was Hawaiian. He was only a fraction Hawaiian, and they don't look much alike, but it was enough. One day several years ago, the morning after a Democratic president was elected, they smiled at one another.

After his walk, Noah bought himself a take-out coffee from Albert Chong at the café in the hotel lobby. It was a long day at the hotel as the manager of three bars. He created the schedules and assigned appropriate shifts for each staff member. Noah prided himself on keeping everyone happy; he had a flair for organizing everyone into workable groups.

Some of the younger staff had come to Hawaii to surf the big winter waves. Noah was always reluctant to talk about surfing. He had seen their slick bottom turns, their fancy air tricks in the shore break, but they had just arrived from Florida, California and Texas. They didn't know better than to ask him about the North Shore, his history with the place.

The pool-side bar had a natural frame with wooden pillars holding up the bamboo roof. The bar itself was shiny red wood. Noah leaned forward on the bar, rested on one elbow. He twirled two shark's teeth on a gold chain around his neck. He wore a casual shirt, not the V-neck shirts the hotel staff wear, but a red-and-white, floral Hawaiian shirt. It was his favourite.

The fall night was unseasonably warm. William was sitting at a table on the patio of the café, waiting for Janis. The framed picture lay wrapped by his side.

After twenty minutes the waiter came over to his table and asked him his name. "There's a Janis on the phone," the waiter said.

"William, the car's broken down. I'm waiting for the tow truck. It could be hours."

"Oh, don't worry, I'll see you later."

"Have something to eat anyway," she said.

The waiter took his order and left.

From across the street, April called out his name. "Hello," she said as she approached. "I don't mean to interrupt … but I just thought I'd come say hi."

"It's all right, I'm alone," he said, wishing he hadn't. "Do you want to sit for a minute?" he managed to say rather casually.

William regarded her long, dark hair. April looked older, more refined. She had her glasses on today, a blue jacket and a necklace that he'd never seen before.

"When did you get that?" he asked, without really meaning to.

"This necklace? I've had it for ages. I bought it at that arts-and-crafts show two years ago. Remember the green bed-spread that you spilled paint on the very next day? I bought them from the same stall. God, I was mad." She smiled and ordered a pint of dark beer.

"I've missed you," he said.

"I broke up with Nathan," she said. "It didn't even last a month."

"I was going to ask you about him."

"Don't bother."

It was too soon to be having this conversation.

"Can I ask you a question?" he said.

"As long as it's not about *us*."

April and William talked about his painting for almost an hour. It was years since they'd discussed art and though there was a time they couldn't agree on anything art related, they chatted easily now about the process, the construction of the finished piece from the parts.

April thought about it for some time and then proposed an idea.

"Take it apart again. No let me. How many sketches did you do?"

"Thirty-six," he said. "But they really were just pieces. Not whole sketches."

"No, I get it. Would you trust me with it, then? I'll complete the same process, and we'll compare my thirty-six with yours."

William watched April leave the café and disappear into the Friday night crowd. Janis would be home by now. When he asked for the bill, he discovered April had already paid it.

Curt sat in the bar at Honolulu International Airport, contemplating how much he hated Americans. Especially the nice ones. He hated how he'd heard of every city in America — Austin, Buffalo, Sacramento, Wichita — but American tourists either tripped over or drew out all the wrong syllables of Melbourne and Brisbane. Why didn't he have the same trouble spitting out Milwaukee or Baltimore? He hated that he could sing a few bars of "The Star-Spangled Banner" and that the beer he was drinking was featured in movies he'd seen. He even recognized the neon advertising in this tacky bar. He'd always hated American politics, American righteousness and American bloody ignorance. He hated American late-night television. And baseball, God he hated baseball.

The magazine on the plane said Hawaii was hot in June and warm in December. *It's your value-added vacation destination of choice.* It was halfway to everywhere he wanted to be.

The woman who'd sat beside him on the plane kept looking over at him from across the bar. She was alone; he was alone. They'd already talked on and off for twelve hours during the flight — more than most people talk to their neighbours over the course of a year. He knew all about her, how *nice* she was. She was an American who worked for the Australian government. Her mother lived with her sister in Chicago. She was going home to surprise them.

"What can I getcha, brah?" The bartender was a young

Hawaiian bloke with dark shoulder-length hair, light brown skin, not unlike his own.

"Coors," he said, pronouncing it like they do on TV. This threw the Australian bloke at the next table off his scent. The man had rightly thought Curt was an Aussie and wanted to start a conversation. The man was disappointed, but Curt refused to be his five-minute friend.

He asked the bartender for a pack of Camel Lights. His fake accent wavered. The bartender didn't seem to notice. The Australian bloke picked it up right away and shot him a look.

Soft rock music was playing over the airport intercom. On the TV above the bar, a network talking head interviewed an actress whose face Curt couldn't place. Even though the sound was off everyone in the bar watched them, watched the way she flicked her blonde hair and laughed as if she's playing the part of herself. He drank his beer and hummed along with the music in the background. He knew the song but couldn't remember who sings it. This was his culture too. He knew America, even though he'd never been here before. And this was only Hawaii.

Curt grew up thinking everything was Australian, even Cornflakes and Fords. Part of becoming an adult in Australia is learning that almost nothing is Australian, that just about everything that's new comes from America, and everything that's old comes from England.

He remembered seeing a BBC documentary not long ago featuring young Australians and Americans who travelled Europe in hordes. First the camera crew followed a group of Australian backpackers roaming across Europe: a pack of half-pissed dingoes, yapping too loudly, planting their nasal accent in the world's cafés, mangy dogs pissing on well-bred flowers.

Then they followed a group of Yanks, who were much the same. Not much of a shock, he'd thought at the time. But trust the smug poms to make it their business to let Australians know their own reputation. No wonder he hated the English.

Curt ordered another beer, this time a Fosters, out of spite. It tasted American. He thought of Kylie at the airport sending him off, her thin-lipped smile, rolled the lighter she'd given him around in his pocket.

William and Janis had made the trip north at the last minute, despite the threat of rain. Now she lay sleeping on the cottage sofa under the broad window that looked out over the lake. The speckled light fell across her face, having bounced off the water and through the pines. She'd been reading for much of the afternoon, classical music floating up from the kitchen radio, but now she slept.

From where William sat across the room, he could see her lips moving slightly as she breathed in and out. She seemed to be singing, softly mouthing the words of a dream.

She'd spent the day reminiscing, running her fingers across the spines of mystery and romance paperbacks she'd read in her teens and over her parents' books, from *their* childhood, books she'd devoured when she was very young: Zane Grey, the Bobbsey Twins, Enid Blyton. She'd read passages aloud from their stiff, sun-dulled pages, characters she'd loved, scenes that had scared her half to death.

Fat drops of rain splashed against the windows. Janis stirred, but did not wake. William wondered about the other men who'd sat in this chair before him, what had been left unsaid this afternoon, what she must have purposely avoided.

The cottage was dim, the afternoon's light flat. William imagined Janis with her hands spread against the window frame, rain on the other side of the glass only inches from her nose, and another man, Robin, behind her. Janis, her face close to the glass, seeing her reflection smeared in the rain drops, the man, his strong hands on her sides, hips, mistaking tears in her reflection for raindrops.

William stepped outside. Fall was in the air, a heavy earthen smell of wet dirt and rotting leaves. He made his way across the lawn to the first large pine tree, halfway down to the water's edge, and leaned against its rough bark, his hand wet and cool. Three seagulls floated close to shore. A light from a cottage across the lake flicked on. It produced a single streak over the surface of the darkening lake. It was useless. None of this meant anything to him.

Curt was on a plane for twenty-four hours, and now he had another twenty in Toronto. He checked in to a hostel downtown. "We're a hellova deal," the man said on the phone. He was so tired he could hardly think straight.

He put his pack on a bed and wandered down into a common room. He ate the lunch provided, washed it down with coffee and met a German girl who invited him to go to the art gallery with her for the afternoon.

Masterpieces filled the first room and the only thing that captured him, held him, was her eyes. Another room, Canadian landscapes of lakes, rivers, pine trees, canoes and rocks. They wandered farther into the gallery and sat in a small booth to listen to an audio recording narrating the tour. He looked at her and she took his hand. She looked shaken. They removed their headphones and when he asked her what was wrong she said, "Friedrich." He patted her shoulder and instinctively drew her near. They headed outside into the cold air. His jumper wasn't heavy enough, but they began to walk through Chinatown anyway, people shopping and bartering and rushing all about them. She was a tall, blond rock jutting out of a short, dark river.

They ate at a Vietnamese restaurant where the waiter couldn't understand his Australian English, so she ordered for both of them in French. There was a ceramic green dragon suspended above their table and Curt realized he had never eaten Vietnamese food before. It wasn't like Chinese food at all.

Her mind was in Berlin, while his own drifted to and from Sydney. Together they were loving their respective lovers. Toronto was Berlin. He was Friedrich. Toronto was Sydney. She was Kylie. Only the warmth of their entwined fingers was real.

They stopped at a faux-English pub nestled into the bottom floor of a highrise office building. The Duke of Somewhere or other was filled with loosened ties and fallen faces, dart boards and coats of arms, ice hockey games on TV screens. She motioned that she wanted to leave. Outside he could see his breath, but the sky was darkening. Pink and blue neon signs advertising fresh bagels and hot coffee swirled in the night. The moon was vast. When they reached the hostel, she said she'd go to her room — he should stop in before he leaves for the airport the next morning.

In the common room, Curt began to write a postcard to his father. Other travellers were making plans, talking.

He went to her room, knocked softly. He opened the door to discover that she'd removed her jeans, but not her socks and the long white shirt she was wearing was unbuttoned and hung to her thighs.

She put her head on his shoulder and they fell back onto the bed.

She'd fallen asleep next to him, her head on his chest, but he was wide awake, Sydney time.

Later Curt realized she was staring at him; far away in Berlin it was morning. He pushed a strand of her hair behind her ear. She closed his burning eyes with her fingers; the air was dry and he felt unbearably tired. She kissed his eyelids so gently she may not have touched them at all. His T-shirt was being pushed up his chest, her hair pulled across his stomach as she moved south with all the slowness and heaviness of the tide. Sleep and drowning merged. He was Friedrich. He was blond, mighty, Teutonic.

What's your name?

She'd fallen asleep.

Will you remember me? Have I mattered?

Someone walked in silhouette in front of a window on the top floor of a house across the street.

Her perfume lingered on his clothes all the way to Spain.

William answered the phone.

"It's me," April said. "Sorry, I know it's late." Muffled crying on the other end of the line. "Can you come over?"

It was one in the morning. A harvest moon lit his way as he thrust his hands deeper into his pockets and walked south, to April's place. It took him forty minutes to navigate the grey depthlessness of changing leaves and dry, cool air.

William sat on the pull-out couch they'd inherited years ago from his parents, the same saggy one he'd slept on for three months before his departure. He looked around the room. It was a warm yellow now and she'd moved the furniture, positioned it the way they'd tried once before but hadn't liked. After a weekend of tripping over the coffee table, they'd moved it all back. April's artwork lined the far wall. Two large pieces he'd never seen before, the others were from years past, ones April couldn't sell or part with.

"It's been six months since you moved out," she said and her hand covered her mouth, rubbed her face.

"I know," William said. "Hard to believe."

"It was great to see you the other day. Thanks for giving me your piece. I haven't had a chance to work on it yet, but I will."

"Why am I here, April?"

"I'm sorry I called you," she said. In the light he could see how red her eyes were. Her dark hair was pulled back; her skin was pale. "Nathan came over tonight," she said. "We had a fight."

"I thought you told me at the café that you'd broken up. Didn't last a month …"

"It *was* over, but he was still living here."

"That sounds familiar."

"I'm so tired," she said as her chin fell to her chest. "I can't sleep."

William stood. He opened up the pull-out couch, picked April up and laid her on the mattress. She fell asleep as he held her.

When he got up to turn off the light, the curtains swayed against the open window and the moon filled the room, lighting her skin. She always left the window open a crack, even in the winter. He closed it quietly. On the street below, a pair of dogs darted into the shadows and the late-night lights of the traveller's hostel burned across the street. He drew the curtains and climbed onto the mattress beside her. He was home.

In the morning William woke to the sound of the shower. He got up, washed the coffee cups and folded up the bed. How many times had he done this?

"Hi," April said emerging from the hallway. She wore black jeans and a loose, grey T-shirt. Her hair was still damp.

"I guess I should go," he said.

"Thanks." She stood tall in the door frame.

He looked at her feet, clear of nail polish and jewellery. "Give me a call," he said, moving to the front door. She walked to him, pulling him to her. Her thumb swept across his cheek, her fingers touched the back of his neck, her lips pressed against his forehead.

Outside in the bright morning, William smelled coffee, eggs, toast, bacon cooking at the restaurant on the corner. He wanted to paint — whites, blues, reds. He felt buoyant. With the tree-lined road stretching north before him and not a car in sight, he started to run. Arms and legs pounding up and down, he was weightless.

He couldn't remember the last time he'd run, the sound of his own breathing, the cool air rushing into his lungs. In a park down the street from his apartment, a father was playing tag with his two boys. Hands on knees, catching his breath, William watched as one little boy squealed and ran behind his father's leg, grabbing it like the trunk of a tree. The other boy leapt onto a nearby swing, laughing uncontrollably as he launched himself into the air and hung for a moment before falling backward. The father laughed, waved at a woman sitting on a bench with a book. William could tell she was not really reading. She pretended to have stolen a well-earned break, but she couldn't take her eyes off her boys for a moment. They were young and still doing and experiencing things for the first time.

Dear Dad:

This postcard's from the art gallery in Toronto, where I had a lay-over before my flight to Madrid. Sorry I didn't get a chance to say goodbye properly before I left. Not sure how long I'll be gone. I've met an English bloke here, Jamie, who invited me to his parents' house on an island in the Mediterranean! Can't say no to that. Hope you're settling into your new place.

Love,
Curt

P.S. Hi to Debbie.

The next day William left work early. He was going to surprise Janis by making dinner. He only had a small kitchenette in his basement apartment, so he would have to use hers. At the grocery store, he bought garlic, basil, olives, oregano, fusilli, plum tomatoes, a French stick and expensive coffee. He stopped in at the liquor store and picked up a bottle of Shiraz and a small bottle of port.

He hadn't seen much of Janis recently. At the beginning of the week, she was busy at an editor's conference, two nights ago she was at her mother's and last night she was working to deadline. With his grocery bags in hand, William walked up the stairs and around the back of the house. If he worked quietly, the smell would greet her before he did.

It was a cool evening, his breath clouding in front of his face. He put the bags on the grass and in the waning light he leaned against the crabapple tree to see through the window. Janis tossed her hair as she floated about the kitchen. There were two windows open and William caught fragments of conversation along with trills and runs of the Vivaldi playing in the background. Hidden safely behind the crabapple, he thought her blue kitchen looked cosy and inviting; Robin would be there for some time.

Robin lit a tall white candle and opened a bottle of champagne that had a very pleasing pop judging from the way Janis laughed and threw her hair back. The lights were dimmed. A toast! Robin leaned in, their glasses touched, Janis looked away, out the window.

William stormed down the stairs into his apartment, stuffed the groceries into the fridge. He could hear them walking around. He thought of phoning her. He opened the port instead. Halfway through the bottle, he remembered the key to Robin's house.

Once inside, William retraced the steps of his first expedition, the antique globe, the impaled horses above Robin's desk. On the fridge this time was a picture of Robin and Janis. *Bastard*. He put the picture in his pocket. He downed a beer and left it in the nook on the landing halfway up the staircase.

Just as he flopped down on the unmade bed, William heard the front door open.

"God, it feels as if I never left."

William climbed into the closet and pulled the door, leaving it slightly ajar. At his feet was the Cellini, untouched. He could hear them climbing the stairs. They didn't stop on the landing. They were giggling.

"Shower?" Robin asked.

"I'll join you in a minute."

Through the crack, not ten feet away from him, William watched Janis light a cigarette and smoke it sitting on the bed. She picked up the phone and whispered, "Hi, William, it's me. Where are you? I had to go to my mother's again tonight. Do you want to grab a late supper? If I don't hear from you, I guess I'll just stay here. Tomorrow, then?" Janis replaced the phone on the cradle and then went into the bathroom. The shower was already running.

The whole thing took forty minutes.

They left together, as quickly as they'd arrived. William waited inside the closet for another few minutes, then picked up the phone beside the bed and dialled Janis' number. He was calm.

"Sorry I missed your call tonight. I was out. Let's have dinner tomorrow."

William jammed his finger down on the receiver. His words had been clear and precise. He replaced the key but this time kept the picture. The Cellini was still in the closet.

Port de Pollença, Mallorca, was quiet just before dawn. With the streets mostly clear — off-season for tourists — the town felt like an abandoned movie set. It was here that, on his way home from The Festa de Sebastia, Curt dropped his lighter down a sealed storm-water drain.

He remembered this for the first time, several hours later, clutching his head, his fingers shading the sun from his eyes. The sunlight bathed his whole body, despite its reduced winter strength. A window beside him stretched from the villa's floor to ceiling. He was trying to sleep in the living room on the carpet, behind the couch. It was a good, private place to suffer. If he opened his eyes, a stretch of blue sea would lay before him. If he opened his eyes now, even gradually, he'd surely throw up.

Late yesterday afternoon they'd wandered into town, sat in an empty restaurant, ate bread and eggs fried in olive oil, washed it all down with beer. They had smoked a few cigarettes and chatted to the waiter, Pedro, whom they'd met several nights ago in a bar. Pedro spoke English with a South African accent, having lived in Johannesburg while on a student exchange a year ago.

"Are you going to Pollença?" Pedro asked, describing the small local festival set to take place later that night.

Jamie, Curt and Rachel, the Scottish woman renting the villa next door, took him up on his invitation.

In the main square, men and women mingled, their children running in circles chasing each other giddily. Actors from the festival still dressed in medieval folk costume were smoking, eating, laughing. Music drifted up from an open doorway leading down a few stairs into darkness.

Inside they found a narrow bar with bare walls and a stage at one end. It was crowded with locals. The room was loud and hot. They wormed their way through the people, looking for a table.

After a few drinks, Curt was on the stage belting out straight twelve-bar blues on a piano so old it may have been Chopin's. The crowd whooped and cheered as he began playing standing up. Pedro joined him on the Spanish guitar, someone else had a bongo, another a trumpet, and they played impromptu half-versions of show tunes, Beatles hits and torch songs. A huge woman in a red dress sang in Spanish, her arms outstretched, the crowd singing along.

Curt drank into the night with Pedro, several farmers, a cop from Madrid, a tour guide from Wales and a French biology student.

He got a lift back to the port on a moped. Just as he was trying to remember his way back to the villa, the Scottish woman, Rachel, called to him from a table outside a small café by the marina. The place was almost empty.

Curt squeezed his eyes shut, afraid to move. The sun on his body, as he tries to remember.

He and Rachel were on their way home on foot, when he dropped his lighter down the drain. It was three feet down, lying in stubby grass. The drain seemed to be unconnected to a larger system. It didn't run anywhere, it was simply a random, grated hole. It was the only drain for miles.

They kissed beside the tennis court, hot, alcohol-slathered breaths. Then behind the couch on the floor of Jamie's villa, in front of the entire Mediterranean, they grabbed drunken handfuls of each other.

His hand was across his face. It was warm. His eyes opened a crack. He was alone. He considered his lighter, the engraving, *A Love Supreme*. He considered that it's almost winter in Mallorca.

William stood at the stove scraping plum tomatoes off the cutting board into the hot saucepan with the onions and garlic. Above his head hung the copper pots. "Wine?" he asked.

Janis was sitting at the harvest table, the newspaper spread out in front of her, pencil in hand, attempting to complete the crossword. "Oh, not for me tonight. Thanks anyway," said Janis.

"It's red."

"No, it's not that ... I had a few drinks last night ... with my mother."

William poured the pasta into the colander, steam rising up in the air, fogging the windows. "How about some music? Put on the Vivaldi. Light a candle."

Janis stood up and went into the other room without saying a word.

The idea to mimic the evening she'd just had with Robin had occurred to him in the closet.

She stood in the doorway to the kitchen kneading her forehead. Her eyes were a dull grey-blue. "I've got a migraine coming on, William."

"Just a minute and I'll rub your temples."

"No. I'm just going to have to lie down. I'm sorry you went to all this trouble."

"Pass me the barbecue tongs," Curt asked Jamie, who was on his hands and knees with a piece of wood and a metal ruler. Jamie looked like he was in prayer, his nose inches from the grate.

It was late afternoon, and they'd walked to the storm-water drain to have a second, more serious, attempt at retrieving the lighter. It glistened, only two feet down. They'd tried tugging at the grate and then improvising with kitchen utensils. Nothing had worked.

Rachel drove by in her rented jeep and pulled over. "Can I give you a hand?" asked Rachel. She looked much older than Curt remembered. Rachel stood behind him, her hand rested on his shoulder. "We could pull it up with the jeep," she suggested.

They tied a rope to the bumper and to the grate. The rope went taut for a moment, then snapped, the grate unmoved.

Several local children rode their bikes over to see what was going on. There was pointing, nodding. An older brother showed up with two metal rods that he tried to manoeuvre like oversized chopsticks.

After about an hour, fifteen people stood around the grate. Some had forgotten why they were there and were talking to neighbours. One man, an engineer, looked down the drain and laughed before walking away. Another car attempted to pull up the grate with a chain. Its wheels spun on the sandy road.

"I don't know what to say about last night," Curt finally said to Rachel in a lull.

"I'm leaving the day after tomorrow anyway." She smiled.

Curt thought he liked her mannerisms, her mouth, her voice. The crowd had suddenly swollen to more than forty. Six cars and three or four dogs milled around the grate. Men argued about how best to tie a rope for a third go at pulling the grate up with a vehicle; women with spatulas, coat hangers, pieces of hose, ropes, spoons and forks jostled for attention; kids chased each other in circles on their bikes, distracted their parents and aggravated the dogs.

A small boy handed out sticks of gum to everyone. Minutes later there were forty people standing around the drain, chewing vigorously.

It worked, of course. The boy collected the gum from everyone's mouth, moulded it to the end of a long shaft of wood, stabbed the alluvial lighter, which dutifully adhered to the gum, and carefully pulled it up through the grate to safety.

Under the circumstances there was nothing left to do but thank everyone and light a cigarette, an act that drew a fine round of applause.

Rachel and Curt walked into town and drank coffee at Pedro's restaurant. They talked. She scribbled down her address on a coaster. "Look me up if you ever get to Dundee."

Later Curt sat at the restaurant alone and looked out over the water. He ordered his first beer of the day. It'd been almost four weeks since he'd left Sydney.

Pedro came over with his beer. "Will you come and play jazz with me tonight in Palma?" he asked.

There had been something accidental about the night before, Curt thought. Something simple, but impossible to recreate. He wondered how could he *write* music that impulsive.

Toronto's first flurry carpeted the grass of the park down the street from Janis and William's place, where they sat rocking back and forth on the swings, their feet dragging on the ground.

William's hands were deep in his pockets. His shoulders hunched, elbows squeezed tightly into his body, stubbly chin pressed down, arms crossed. His right leg twitched. Across the park the bench — wooden slats, concrete — was unoccupied save for a seagull.

When Janis got up to leave, she did so without William. He watched her leave footprints behind in the snow. Then she was gone. The snow fell a little heavier and her tracks were covered within the hour. The park was illuminated by a single streetlight and stretched out before William like a canvas whitewashed. He wanted to leave it that way, unmarked, unspoiled, but there was no way to get home without walking across it. He was stuck in the middle, suspended on a swing.

The inter city express pulled out from the platform in Madrid, bound for Paris. Curt had only managed three days in Madrid; the city made him lonely, made him think seriously about his mother. He had called Aunt Jilly to see how she was getting on. She mentioned Kylie had been round to check up on her the day before.

In his compartment two American men discussed their schedule. One told the other it was a fifteen-hour trip. Curt had been the last of four passengers to cram in. Both the Americans had laptop computers; one was already typing. The woman across from Curt glanced at him and rolled her eyes. She had been trying to read but she'd given up; the tapping was too distracting. She produced a baguette and a bottle of wine from her luggage. "Would anybody like some wine?" She was French.

Curt took a paper cup half full. One of the Americans thanked her, but said they had their own, and then promptly produced a beer.

"I'm Monique," she said.

Curt shook her hand and introduced himself to the two Americans.

As the train rolled farther away from Madrid, the warm sun set on a winter's day and cast the Spanish countryside in a rusty red. Curt dozed off. Monique talked to the two Americans, but seemed bored. They *were* boring, Curt thought. He caught only fragments of their conversation amid the noise of the train and his slippery dreams. He woke up an hour later and dug out his pen and paper.

Dear Kylie,

I'm on a train from Madrid to Paris, a tiny compartment, four of us crammed in here for five hours. Thankfully two American passengers just moved to new seats, so it's just me and an older French woman now.

I've been in Mallorca for the past few weeks, off the coast of Spain. I don't think I'm going to stay in Paris for long. Going to head straight to England instead. For some reason I'm tired of being a foreigner.

When I was walking around the streets in Madrid (in one museum or another), I'd see a shop or a book or a painting and think "Oh Kylie would love that." The way we left things — half on, half off — was confusing.

I've been trying not to think about Mum. I wish that they hadn't worked, the pills I mean. I wish that she'd lived so I could tell her how fucking mean it was to ask me to forgive her.

I've decided to investigate my birth family when I get to England. What do you reckon? All I know is that I was born in London. I'll see what I can find out. I'll need to go to some sort of agency, I guess.

I'll write another soon.

Love,

Curt

Monique sat diagonally across from Curt. She read with a tiny light attached to the top of her book. The compartment door was locked. It was dark. The train swung in a smooth, gentle, back-and-forth rhythm. His eyes were closed, but he wasn't asleep. They both stretched out their legs on the seat opposite. She shifted around slightly, trying not to wake him up, and although he wasn't asleep he appreciated her consideration. He opened his right eye to a slit, almost accidentally, to find she'd turned off her light, put her book down, spread a blanket over her lower half. Her eyes were closed. A light from a farmhouse or passing car occasionally illuminated her face.

Christmas was just five days away. William's mother had called him twice to make sure he'd be home for the holidays. He'd been thinking about last Christmas, April, how she'd cooked a turkey. He hadn't heard from her in weeks.

"April?"

"William?" she said. Her voice was surprised, rushed.

"Hi, how are you? Merry Christmas," he said.

"Oh, William, listen, I can't talk now. I'm late for a train. I'm going to Montreal on business. I've been meaning to call you. I know it's short notice, but are you free on Boxing Day for dinner?"

"Sure, that'd be nice. Thanks."

He hung up, pulled on his coat and headed out into the December night. The smell of the neighbours' fires — cedar and pine — filled his senses.

The night before he and Janis had exchanged gifts: a fountain pen for her, a leather backpack for him. Last month they'd agreed to end it, just be friends. It seemed best.

On Christmas Eve William sat in his old bedroom, now his father's study, complete with matching desk, filing cabinets, credenza, cream walls and green twill carpet. His mother had completely redecorated, right down to the staplers and in-baskets. His father stood back in the doorway, apologizing for the apparent extravagance.

"You'll be sleeping in the basement," said his mother.

"I'm going to build a new room down there, beside the furnace. A guest bedroom," said his father. "You'll have somewhere proper to stay next time."

In the evening his mother went off to Christmas mass. William and his father put on their jackets and went out on the back deck. It was still above zero with no sign of more snow.

"Cheers," said William as his father handed him a beer. "Backyard looks good."

"Does, doesn't it."

"How's work?"

"It's been tough. Remember Bill Lowe? Sure you do, bear of a fellow, red beard, VP National Sales and Co-Branding? He was on the retail-development side. Got the sack. Just like that. Been with the company for nineteen years. Started on the floor of the first plant we opened outside the U.S. Christ, he used to work for old man Derwent himself. But you've got to make the numbers. That's all there is to it."

"That's tough," said William, taking a sip. "Ever worry you'll be next?"

"Some days. There's talk Pittsburgh might be cutting off the Canadian arm. Move it down to Mexico. Cheaper. Better leverage, bigger margins — I've seen the numbers. It's hard to blame the firm. Still. Imagine throwing together a résumé at Bill's age."

His father walked off the patio and strolled around the yard in silence. He was a tall, lean man. He reached up to the fence to remove a fallen branch. "It's hard to keep this yard in good shape. It'll be the death of me."

His father resumed his position leaning on the porch railing next to William. "I decided to get a dog. Something to keep your mother company during the day, a bulldog. She used to have a British bulldog years ago."

"She had a bulldog on the farm?"

"No, when she was … in England."

"Oh, yeah, I always forget she used to live there. What was the name of the school where she taught?" asked William, finishing his beer.

"Don't ask me. Her either. It'll set her off. Things are difficult enough. Listen, it's a surprise Christmas present."

"I'm sure she'll love it."

"A couple of months ago, she didn't even get out of bed — I mean for the whole month. We've been going to a doctor together since then — twice a week."

"I didn't realize things were that bad."

"Well, you never come home anymore. She misses you."

William looked down at the manicured garden beds.

They went back inside. When his father left to pick up the dog, William grabbed another beer from the refrigerator and went into the living room to watch TV. He thought about taking a walk down to the park, to the lake, but decided against it.

"Ruth?" His father was coming in the side door, keys rattling.

"Roger? We're in the living room. Do you need a hand, darling? Where were you?"

William stood and turned off the TV. He winked at his mother, who looked a little bit puzzled. His father appeared at the door cradling a blanket.

"Oh, Roger. What's wrong?" said his mother, leaping to her feet.

"Merry Christmas," Roger said, holding the blanket out to her.

For the next hour, Ruth sat on the recliner, stroking the puppy, murmuring, thanking them, crying a little. "I know I'm not supposed to," she began, "but I'd like a weak gin and tonic, if you don't mind."

"I think we could manage that," said Roger, standing. "I can't remember the last time you had a drink anyway." He left the room and went downstairs to the bar.

"You were just four when you first came to live with us," Ruth said, talking to William but looking at the sleeping puppy. "You were staying with my mother on the farm for a week while we moved into the new house. Your father picked you up and brought you home. You'd been asleep in the car, so he picked you up and carried you in — still sleeping. Tonight was just like that."

His mother stroked the dog, its pink tongue poking out the side of its mouth, eyes squinting. She kept looking down at the dog and then back up at William.

"Merry Christmas, Mom," he said, walking over to her and kissing her on the top of her head. She smiled, nodded, looked down at the puppy in her arms.

"One weak gin and tonic and two beer," said Roger, entering the room. "It's after midnight. Merry Christmas. Here's to the four of us."

Curt spent a week in London trying to find his birth parents, but with so little to go on he had no success. He stayed at dirty youth hostels and spent a miserable Christmas day with three New Zealanders. He was becoming impatient and he was about to ring an old family friend, Beatrice Litton, when he decided to contact Rachel in Scotland instead. He would visit Beatrice to collect any forwarded mail, but he would head north first.

"I'm glad you came," Rachel said on the way home from the station.

"You sure?"

"You'll be a great excuse to take a long weekend."

After a walk around Dundee, they decided on a drive into the countryside.

"This is where the Queen Mother grew up," said Rachel as they made their way down the long tree-lined driveway toward Glamis Castle.

From the outer wall and gates, with its beasts and satyrs, Glamis appeared to Curt to be a series of medieval office towers, a city skyline from a time gone by. Its stonework looked pinkish in the distance, but up close the stone darkened.

Curt was struck by how small Scotland was — that this fairy-tale castle could exist so close to bank machines, to industry. He walked by row upon row of stuffed deer heads, swords, shields and mounted armour. He listened to the legends that accompanied each Flemish painting, every Jacobean chair.

Curt considered Australia, its history and his own. He knew people at home who could count five or six generations in the same shire. Some had direct bloodlines to convict stock. His mother's flat was in a house built in 1905. Scotland's was a history before Australia had begun. White Australia, anyway. He remembered the Celtic weave etched into the sandstone pillar, Kylie's fingers tracing its pattern, Shark Island asleep in the harbour.

They joined a walking tour. Curt stood in a small chapel on one side of Glamis Castle.

"In 1688 a Dutch artist, Jacob de Wet, was commissioned by the third Earl of Strathmore to paint this series of religious panels," the guide began. "De Wet felt he was not paid enough money for this important commission, so on completion he asked the earl for additional money but was refused. Enraged, the artist stole into the chapel and painted a large black hat on the figure of Christ. It is, I'm told, the only known depiction of Jesus wearing a hat."

Religious scenes painted on walls and ceilings covered every portion of the small chapel: *The Last Supper*, *The Flight into Egypt*, *St. Andrew*. Curt recalled the cubist stained glass in the church at his mother's funeral. It was so different in style from this chapel. He wondered how they could both be for the same God.

From the chapel they walked on to the billiard room, the great hall, the royal apartments, the crypt, Duncan's hall. Oil paintings loomed over him, eyes belonging to people who had likely never seen a person with brown skin like his; their armour, ancestral china, personalized silver hallmarks, familial embroideries, coats of arms and tartans made Curt feel small and foreign.

After the tour Rachel and Curt headed farther north. She told him that she sold insurance in Dundee, that her car was new this year. She telephoned her office on her car phone and asked her assistant to book her a room at a hotel in Aviemore.

"It's a ski resort," she said. "We'll pay too much, but there should be something to do tonight."

He'd been a guest, a traveller, a tourist, for so long he didn't remember what it was like to spend a day without having to pay for the privilege of leisure or be grateful to people for their hospitality.

In the car he thought about the night he and Rachel had spent together in Mallorca. He remembered only glimpses of her body. He looked at her arm on the steering wheel, how it was straight and taut. Her hair was still dark, but it was shorter now. It suited her better.

She slid in a jazz tape, John Coltrane. The Scottish highlands slipped by outside, and he thought Australia was a long way off. The trees were different, the villages were like nothing he'd ever seen, but changing geography hadn't helped him. Travelling was not a licence to lie. He was becoming more and more lost.

They decided to pick up a picnic lunch and eat it on the out-skirts of a village, not far from Blair Castle. Rachel stopped the car under some trees. There were two small houses in the dis-tance, smoke from the chimneys, a forest not far off.

The path was wide and well worn, likely by children riding their bikes. Rachel took Curt's hand and led him, through thicker growth. The faint path opened up to a small clearing.

The deer standing in the centre darted off. It was small, fragile, its cloven hooves visible as they padded softly away across the grass.

He lay back on the thick tartan blanket and looked up at the blue sky — they could be anywhere, but he was sure it was somewhere Rachel had been with other men. Their breath appeared in bursts, the blue air, green ring of trees, Rachel, everything fell away into a circle, an oval, hollow. The soft remnants of Mallorca dissolved under a cool Scottish sun. *Could I survive here?*

"Look, the deer," she said.

Its nose twitched, its hoof knocking the ground twice, before it pranced off again.

William glanced up at April's ceiling. A jagged crack had opened up in the white plaster like a bolt of black lightning. April cleared away the dishes and William chose a new CD. She insisted on Christmas music. He picked the Bing Crosby, but put it on softly.

April had decorated the artificial Christmas tree they'd bought years ago at The Bay with strings of thin silver beads and white flashing lights. They sat down in front of it — William on the bean bag chair, April cross-legged on the floor — and exchanged gifts. She was the first to get hers open: paints and brushes.

"You're going to laugh when you open yours," she said.

"Well, we always need 'em." He smiled, looking down at his own set.

She tossed her dark hair back and the little lights on the Christmas tree danced across her skin in soft hues. They'd fallen asleep together on the pullout couch last month. Now it was closed, across the room. He recalled the harvest moon.

"Hey, listen," she said. "This might not be the best time to talk to you about this, but it's been on my mind, so I hope you'll hear me out."

"Sure, what's up?" he managed.

"Remember at the café in the summer, when I told you I had a new job? Well, I've started my own graphic design company — Tanaka Design. Easy stuff mostly, letterhead, business cards, logo sketches, whatever comes along really. Mainly computer stuff. I'm the only employee, but the money is good. I end up working long hours, but it's worth it."

William nodded. He watched her long hair swing about as she turned her head, her smile, dark eyes, her feet, her toes, her black jeans, the ones she used to slide off before getting into the shower, before they made love on the bed that used to be theirs. He thought of the mirror on the dressing table where he used to watch her, out the corner of his eye, how she used to like it when he grabbed her feet and ran his fingers up her legs, across her back, lowering her down onto the bed, her mouth talking, still, talking …

"Business was pretty slow for the first few months. Now I'm starting to get too many clients. I think by this summer … well, I guess you know where this is headed. William, I'm looking for a partner."

"What?"

"I mean, I think you'd be a perfect partner, for the business."

He took a mouthful of wine.

"Look, we trust each other," she continued. "We know each other. We're both good artists and we respect each other's work. Think of how much we've grown. Now that we know what we want, we shouldn't abandon each other." She paused.

He remained silent looking down at her feet.

"Maybe I shouldn't have brought this up tonight. What do you think? It's not until the summer, but what's your initial reaction?"

William looked to the ceiling. Black lightning. Outside the snow squalls beat against rattling window.

Before William left April gave him one last present.

Open it up when you get home, she'd said.

As he tore away the paper, he recognized her reconstruction of Janis, mounted behind glass. But it wasn't Janis.

It was him.

The original line of Janis' thigh had become his cheekbone, the arch of her foot was his eyebrow. April had built his portrait from the shards of Janis.

April was all William could think of for days. She was on his mind as he fought his way through the snow on New Year's Eve. "It's awful out there," he said coming into the back of the shop.

"Want a coffee? Philip's coming back soon," Francisco said.

At eleven thirty Philip arrived with sandwiches. When they'd all taken their seats, Philip began, "William, Francisco and I have been thinking about your future. We want to thank you for telling us that you are considering working with April next summer. We know you need new challenges and given that we're getting older ourselves, we've come up with a proposal."

"Wait for it!" said Francisco, reaching for an egg salad sandwich.

"We'd like you to consider becoming a partner in the business," continued Philip. "We're thinking of retiring in the next five years, maybe moving to Italy. We're not sure yet. But we think, in that time, we could teach you to run the place yourself. We could cut you in on the profits so that you'll have enough to buy us out completely in ten years."

William took a tuna sandwich from the tray and looked around, avoiding both Philip's and Francisco's eyes. He'd worked for them for six years. He felt rather numb. He chewed on his sandwich. "My mother's been sick, as you know, and then there's April's proposition. Now this."

"Well, we don't need an answer today," said Francisco, deflated.

"No, just take some time to think it over," added Philip.

"You *are* going to have to make some choices and there will be compromises, but make sure they are *your* compromises. That's the only advice I can give you."

Francisco walked around the table and put a hand on Philip's shoulder, tucking a loose strand of grey hair behind his partner's ear.

Rachel pulled back the curtains in their hotel room to reveal snow-covered mountains. "I always feel like I can see farther up here," she said.

"I went to Mount Kosciusko once on a school excursion," said Curt. "That's the only other time I've seen snow."

After dinner they walked through Aviemore, hand in hand. Curt listened while Rachel told him a story about her father. They heard music coming from a church, so they wandered toward it.

There were people mingling outside under clouds of pipe and cigarette smoke, holding pints of dark beer. Deep laughs competed with the sound of bagpipes coming from inside. Up close they realized that the church was now a pub.

The room was packed. They just managed to squeeze inside. Rachel shuffled down to the bar and ordered them each a pint, while Curt squirmed over to the other side of the room and leaned against a wall. A singer on the stage performed a traditional Scottish song.

When Rachel arrived she was chuckling into her beer. "This is put on for tourists. A Scottish variety show. I'm sorry … I had no idea."

Over the course of the event, several pipers played, two Scottish girls performed what Curt took to be a highland fling and a man dressed up in peasant clothes read a Robbie Burns poem.

The après-ski crowd was full of English university students, healthy German tourists and a long table of rosy-cheeked Japanese honeymooners. There wasn't a sober person in the smoke-filled place and they were too busy enjoying themselves to care about cultural authenticity.

"I was married for two years," Rachel told Curt between songs. "I was still in university. Hamish. Died in a car accident, driving drunk."

"I'm sorry," Curt said. A piper began to play *The Skye Boat Song* Curt's mind drifted.

"But that was twelve years ago," Rachel said, forcing a smile.

"How old are you?" Curt asked.

A drummer joins the lone piper on the stage.

"Thirty-six."

After the piper and drummer ended their duet, they heard the hum of an electric guitar being plugged in. On the stage a tall, thin man with a long beard and a narrow face placed his bony fingers on the neck of a guitar. Behind him loomed a huge arched window. The man was wearing a broad, black hat.

"It's Jesus," said Rachel suddenly, laughing. "From the paintings in the chapel at Glamis. Jesus of Aviemore."

They were drunk.

Rachel and Curt stumbled back along the road into the village. The night was cold, but they talked and laughed all the way up the elevator into the hotel, all the way into the room, all the way into bed.

The next day they drove farther north, to Nairn. Cawdor Castle looked miniature in comparison to Glamis. They arrived early in the afternoon, hungover, and spent most of the time in the manicured gardens.

"You don't have to come with me to my parents' house tonight if you don't want to," Rachel said.

"You don't want me to come?" Curt asked.

"It might … confuse them." Rachel turned and looked at Curt. He lit a cigarette, slipping Kylie's gold lighter back into his pocket. "My parents are getting old. This has been lots of fun, but … well, I don't want to give them the wrong impression."

Rachel dropped Curt off at the train station in Aberdeen. She smiled the same smile she did in Mallorca and, for a moment, they were standing by the storm-water drain in front of the tennis courts, the warm Mediterranean night around them.

"Happy new year," were the last words she spoke to him.

On the train a passenger across the aisle said something about Hadrian's Wall; it's the last thing Curt recalled before waking up in London. Dreams of swords and deer heads still loomed about him. As he disembarked, the idea of looking for his birth parents seemed less and less likely.

JONATHAN BENNETT

William got home after work and fell onto his futon. He could hear Janis upstairs talking to her mother, Mrs. Oliphant. They were in the kitchen preparing food for the party they were having that night. He and Janis had talked more often in the past few weeks, though cordially. She'd invited him to the party in an awkward moment. Perhaps he should go upstairs and offer to help.

When he entered her kitchen, he walked into cheese plates, shrimp dip, salads, pretzels, sandwiches, cold chicken and bread rolls.

"Barbie Paterson will bring two casseroles — tuna, the best of last year, and a beef," Mrs. Oliphant was saying to Janis. "June Elliot is bringing the desserts, store bought, and Harry and Margot Dupuis are bringing the wine."

Janis had prepared William for what to expect. "Retirees mainly and a whole bunch of my mother's friends and their children and their children's children. Thirty people, perhaps," she'd said. "They come at about four o'clock. Before it gets too dark, because some of them are getting old and have a long drive. The Dupuises come from Niagara-on-the-Lake. Can you believe it? All that way. Most of them leave early, before midnight anyway, because of the drive."

Once he'd been introduced, they put William to work peeling vegetables.

"How did you enjoy the cottage, William?" asked Mrs. Oliphant.

"It was great."

"It's very old, that cottage. Charles was still working for the government when we bought it, shortly after we moved to Toronto. Can you do these carrots too?" asked Mrs. Oliphant.

William peeled and julienned the carrots. The CBC news was on in the background. It was a yearly roundup of important Canadian events.

"I taught kindergarten for forty years. Janis likes children too, really wants some of her own. She used to be a camp counsellor."

"Mom! Enough," said Janis re-entering the room with a bottle of wine and pouring her mother and William each a glass. She looked out the window to the frozen backyard, the bare crabapple tree. "Mom, why don't you go and get ready?"

Mrs. Oliphant left the room.

"Sorry about that," said Janis, leaning into William. "Are you sure you're comfortable being here?"

"Sure," he said.

"Listen, Robin and I have been talking over the past few months ... about getting back together. You see, we never *actually* got divorced. Every year or so we go through this dance thinking maybe we can make it work."

"You told me that you hadn't talked to him in years."

"I tell everyone that. So does he. Our friends want to support us, but make us feel like we're letting them down if we keep running back to each other. I'm sorry. I got married just after I turned nineteen. I was so young."

"Well, what does this have to do with me? We're not

together anymore." William stopped chopping and looked at Janis.

"Robin and I are having a baby. William, I'm pregnant. I thought you should know."

"Is he coming here tonight, to the party?"

"No, Mom's not ready to see him yet. She's still digesting the news."

"I'll bet."

Mrs. Oliphant returned to the kitchen and announced that the snow-covered driveway had to be shovelled. Outside the snow sparkled as the light refracted in pink, orange and blue. William worked his way up and down the path, clearing the snow in clean, straight lines.

"William? They'll be here soon," Janis called him from the doorway. "Could you come inside so I can show you where everything is to fix the drinks?" Her hair was pulled back. In the winter light, her eyes faded from blue to a grey, like her mother's.

"I'll be right there," he said.

After he cleared the path, William made his way across the snow to a large pine tree in the front yard, leaning against its rough bark. His hand was wet, red and cool from shovelling. He regarded the ice that had built up along the eaves-troughs on the old house in crystalline spikes. It was almost dark when he turned and headed back inside.

Jilly sat in her wicker chair. At precisely the same time as she witnessed the intense Australian sunrise, she heard the bell across the field in the school's clock tower give its single ring. The early morning was hot, dry and the first of the new year.

Through the screen on the back verandah, she kept watch over Curt's old high school. He'd been so close for those few adolescent years and, whether reflex or instinct, she continued to look for, to single out, his brown face among the other boys eating lunch on the hill.

Jilly remembered the grey New Year's Day that began 1966. By that time she'd been living in London for six months. She'd gone with Margaret and Ruth for a walk in Battersea Park even though it had been closed. They'd needed fresh air after the festivities of the evening before. As they strolled across the dull grass, laughing, it rained a thin mist.

"Jilly, I think you like that American boy, Noah," said Margaret.

"I think you do too," added Ruth.

"She does like him. I can tell," began Margaret. "Your hands, Jilly," her steely voice suddenly modulating to a belittling tone, "you wring them. And the floor! The floor becomes so interesting when he's talking to you. And where did you both disappear to?"

"Yes," added Ruth. "Where *did* you disappear to?"

"Nowhere," said Jilly flatly. "We sat and chatted. He's just a friend. Besides, he's three years younger than I am. I like to listen to him tell stories about the ocean, about Hawaii. That's all."

Ruth began to push Margaret on an old swing set. Jilly stood to the side and held on to one of the cold, metal poles as the rain fell harder, rolling down into her eyes and mouth.

The night before, Jilly, Margaret and Ruth went down to the pub to usher in the new year. They were the only foreign teachers employed at the school and they lived together in a nearby flat — Jilly and Margaret both Australians, Ruth a Canadian. Circumstance and convenience had initially pressed them together, but eventually they'd formed a kind of friendship.

As soon as Jilly walked into the pub, Noah appeared beside her, smiling, obliging, sipping his scotch. He'd been there for some time drinking with several other American boys. Ruth, Margaret and Jilly joined them, but after an hour Jilly and Noah slipped away and sat together at the table in the corner.

Jilly's eyes passed over Noah's long, dark hair; it had never, in the four times they'd been together, seemed as clean as it was tonight. While she'd been getting ready — putting on Ruth's lipstick, brushing out knots, looking herself over in the mirror — she'd quietly hoped he would show up. Now she wished she'd taken more time.

"There is a point of land on the North Shore of Oahu," Noah began, interrupting her thoughts. "Sometimes the winter sea is flat. On an overcast day with no sunlight, no sound on the beach, the sea runs all the way out to meet the horizon like a single piece of slate. But on other days, when the sun shines, when the wind swings around to offshore and the girls are out with their transistor radios, I go down to Sunset Beach.

The sea ripples its way out like a deep blue corduroy shirt that you can reach and touch with your hand, run your fingertips across the waves, rippling over the bumps. It's like the world was made only for you and you are the only one in it."

How quickly a young woman can fall in love, thought Jilly as she rose from the wicker chair and went into the kitchen to make tea. She used to sing along with the radio when she was young, tapping out the rhythms on Noah's chest, her head resting in the crook of his arm, late into the night. The sound of the rain on the windowsill as they lay smoking cigarettes, trying to be quiet, radio on low. She'd try to sleep, press her body against his so that it protected her even in deep sleep and freed her to dream. She slept so lightly now.

How quickly Noah descended, how he took her down with him, clinging to his chest, and the brown skin on his arm, how it resisted ever so slightly before the needle slid inside. The tracks, the thin leather strip. The money gone on his fix, how her stomach had roared for potatoes, a chop, eggs, some chicken, sausage, her mother's Christmas cake. Some nights she'd wanted relief so badly she'd planned to steal from the shop on the corner. Just a loaf of bread, a can of baked beans. How close she'd come to wanting Noah's escape for herself. *Give me some, just a try.*

If not for the boys. If not for them, she would have, surely.

Noah's phone number was on a letter he wrote to Jilly seven years ago. The letter was still in the back of her recipe book. She flattened out the paper now, the handwriting on it, firm and sharp. Her fingers dialled, number after number. She cleared her throat to project her wobbly voice across the corduroy sea to Noah in Hawaii.

"Hello. Do you have a Noah Lopez working there still? You do? May I speak to him? Thank you. Noah? Yes, it's me. It's nice to hear your voice too. Yes, I'm well. No, the boys are okay. There is some news, though. Curt's in Europe travelling. Just like we were. Yes. No, that's not all. It's, well, it's awful. Margaret died ... Noah, she took her own life. Pills. Two months ago. No. No. He's okay ... just wanted to travel, get away I think. Yes, he's written me a letter. Well, that's why I'm calling. I called Ruth to let her know about Margaret, but she's not well herself. I spoke to Roger instead. Husband, you remember him? Yes, he gave me William's address. Toronto. Well. No, don't call. Write a letter. Give it time to sink in. Don't tell them everything at once. Noah, please leave me out of it. I'll give you William's address. No, send Curt's to me and I'll forward it. Okay. I'll give you an address in London. Beatrice's. Yes, Beatrice's. Yes, we've kept in close ... Okay I'll wait. Ready? Did you get all that? Noah, will you call me and let me know when ... what their reaction is? Thank you. Please do. Resolution. No, you're right. That sounds funny the way ... your accent, that's all. Yes, I will. Thank you. Goodbye."

Jilly put the kettle on the hot plate. She folded up Noah's letter and put it in her recipe book. She made a pot of tea, let it steep, poured a cup, took it out to the verandah, sipped it and looked up at the empty school.

As Noah replaced the phone on the wall, a customer pulled up a stool and rested his elbows on the bar. "Gin and tonic. Lime, lots of ice, please and thanks," he said to Noah with a smile. "You know ... I could be anywhere right now."

Noah half-filled the man's glass with ice, smiled at him.

"This could be Florida," the man said, adjusting his glasses. "I've been to Florida. Barbados, the Dominican, Portugal, the Barrier Reef, California. The wife and I go somewhere hot *every* winter. Not like some people. Never take the same holiday twice, I always say. So me and Helen, we pick somewhere nice from the travel pamphlets in the agency and we're off. You know ..." he paused briefly to sip his drink, "... I think you gotta have faith if you never do the same thing twice. Don't you?"

Noah was counting change. He looked up from the cash register and smiled, shrugging just a little as the man's wife arrived to ask her husband to accompany her shopping.

Noah looked down at the piece of paper — the addresses for his two boys. His hands were shaking.

"I live in Leeds now. Born in London, though. Hardly get there anymore. My sister lives there still with her husband. The wife hates him. Snob he is, with his fancy car. They holiday in France, on the coast. Not like here though, mate. Blue sky, brown women."

Noah nodded and smiled again.

The British man was the last to leave. The pool-side bar was empty and evening was approaching. Noah began to clean up. He wiped down the bar top in his customary long, even strokes as though waxing a surfboard. He collapsed the umbrellas at the tables. These days the occupancy rate was high, the weather was hot and the bar was full. He mixed daiquiris and mai tais, opened lots of Cokes, the odd beer, poured ice water for the swimmers. The outdoor bar beat the aggressive air conditioning of the cocktail lounge or the drunks at the piano bar in the lobby.

Noah stood at the window and looked up Waikiki beach to Diamond Head in the distance. The lights from the hotels mingled as they were cast onto the blackening sea.

He was staying in a room on the nineteenth floor. His boss wanted Noah around in case anything went wrong on the night shift, but he rarely made it back to the North Shore these days, didn't surf much anyway.

Years ago, on big winter days, Noah was often seen on his board sliding out of hollow waves like a man being reborn — but that was before the crowds. It had become unsafe; every other wave some fool dropped in, wiped out, tourists nearly drowned.

For the past fifteen years, Noah had surfed by himself. There were a few spots where he'd be left alone. He went first thing in the morning or after sunset. He told the young surfers on staff he quit long ago, too cold for his old bones. Still, they wanted to hear his stories.

In the early 1960s, he was a young, anonymous teenager, hanging around the North Shore. During the five years he was in England, times had changed — professional surfing had arrived. Foreigners and mainlanders everywhere.

Only a few men on the North Shore knew of Noah, knew that he still surfed. One was a surfboard shaper who lived in, and worked out of, his garage. He made only a few boards a year, gave them away to surfers like Noah. The old man was in his late seventies now, used to dive for black coral. He predicted the surf days ahead of time, knew the sea, reefs, swells, tides and currents better than anyone.

Only half a dozen surfers still knew about this old man, went to him for advice or confession or a plain white surfboard. At one time he was an institution, a living legend, but that had long faded. Noah's father had almost been forgotten, not unlike Noah himself.

Tonight, as Noah lay on the hotel bed, he didn't regret that he wasn't attending the birthday party for another staff member in the lobby piano bar. Ribs. Beer. There would have been lots of people Noah knew.

In his underwear and a white T-shirt, he walked out onto the balcony and took a deep breath of Pacific night air. He was ready. Back in the room, he placed two pieces of hotel stationery side by side on the desk. In front of him was an old colour snapshot of a man, woman and two little boys beside a tree. To his right was a scratch pad covered in illegible scribbles, words buried in ink and moonlight. Finally Noah turned on the desk light, picked up the pen and began to write.

After two more miserable weeks in London struggling to find information about his birth parents, Curt, defeated, called on Beatrice Litton. She immediately invited him to stay.

He arrived at her flat after midnight. She'd arranged with the porter to let him in. The hall light was on. He was greeted only by a little note on the hall stand, his name on it in wobbly handwriting. He was instructed to stay in the first bedroom on the left.

Looking for the bathroom, Curt tiptoed down the hall to the kitchen and followed it out into the living room. The smell struck him first, a mixture of rose and lavender and lemon wood polish, like his mother used ... used to use.

Curt flicked on a lamp that shed frail light into the far corners of the room. Dark English oak furniture, a sideboard that looked longer than two coffins end to end, a nineteenth-century organ in the corner, white lace doilies, Wedgwood, an inkstand, two glass-fronted bookcases filled with leather-bound volumes, peacock feathers, an old globe (Africa just three colours), a tribal mask, crystal decanters, Victorian oil paintings in gold frames, a silver tea set. And asleep on a wingback chair — a huge bulldog. Curt turned off the lamp, its light fading in his eyes, and he headed back to his bedroom without finding the toilet.

"Now you'll have tea, won't you?" Beatrice hovered at the end of Curt's bed.

He stole a glance at the wind-up clock ticking away on the bedside table: six-thirty. "Tea. Yes, please," Curt finally managed, slowly waking. "Tea would be lovely."

She shuffled out of the bedroom, leaving the door open.

Curt heard her somewhere down the hall. After dressing, he found his way to the kitchen and watched Beatrice, a waif of a woman with silver, wavy hair, scuttling about from cupboard to cupboard. "May I use your bathroom?" he asked in his most gentrified Australian accent.

Beatrice, however, didn't seem impressed and continued to measure the spoonfuls of tea into the pot.

He asked again, this time a little louder and a little more affected. Still nothing. Just as he concluded that the old woman was deaf, the bulldog bounded into the kitchen.

She pushed the dog away and motioned Curt to the table. She looked at him up close for the first time. "An earring! Sir Walter Raleigh wore an earring. Delightful! Now come, sit, drink. You'll have to shout, because I'm deaf as a post." She was shouting a little herself.

"Okay," Curt said in a raised voice. "May I use your bathroom?"

"Laugh whom?"

"Bathroom. Toilet."

"There's one in your room, dear."

Curt smiled and backed out of the kitchen. The door in the corner of his room, which he assumed led to a closet, was a small bathroom. On the wall there was an odd pencil drawing of two young women, girls really, caught in rather compromising positions. Both wore expressions of mischievous jubilation.

"Sugar?" she asked, as he re-entered the kitchen.

"Thanks," Curt replied, holding a finger up.

"Here's your mail, dear," she said passing him several envelopes.

"Thanks."

"You must go to St. Paul's."

"Oh, I will," Curt said, leafing through the five or six envelopes she had handed him.

"I used to board foreign teachers for the school. Jilly, Margaret and Ruth lived here. Well, Jilly moved for a time, of course." She pottered about the kitchen for another few moments before adding, "Jilly was so beautiful, you know."

"Yes," Curt said, not knowing where this was going. "I have a letter from Jilly here, I see."

"How is that Noah? Do you ever see him?"

"Who?" Curt asked.

"Noah," she said.

The woman must be senile. "Did you say Margaret lived here?" he asked, changing the subject.

"Yes, my word. And Ruth."

They drank their tea and chatted for ten minutes before Curt excused himself to read his mail in his room.

Mosman, Sydney

Curt:

I realize you're old enough to make your own decisions, but when are you going to start using your head? Right when everyone needs you most, you leave. Jilly has been beside herself. Call her and tell her you are okay.

Thank you for your postcard, but as your father, under the cir-

cumstances, I think a call before your departure would have been more appropriate. Your behaviour is a little erratic, mate. Take some time and think about your responsibilities.

That said, I hope you are having a good time.

— Dad

Curt folded up his dad's letter and placed it back in the envelope. He could hear Beatrice talking to the bulldog as she prepared its food.

Coogee, Sydney

Curt,

I don't know when you'll get this or if you'll write back (I'll understand if you don't.) I just want you to know that I'm missing you and that I hope when you get back we can give it another try.

I went round and saw Jilly last week and we had a good old chat.

I received your letter written on the train to Paris. I think of you all the time — am reminded by the littlest things, like how you hate radishes. It feels like they're all I've eaten lately. As if I'm trying to get in a lifetime's supply while you're gone.

Your mates in the band say hi. I went round to the pub to see them last Friday. See what you're doing to me?

Tonight I can hear the Coogee Bay Hotel. It's hot. I watched the cricket (for about five minutes) today in your honour. Somebody even got out. India was playing Australia in a one-day match. I think.

Work is boring, no one to complain about it to.

I had Giovanni's tonight. There's almost three-quarters of a pizza in the fridge in tin foil. Come home and eat it.

— Kylie

"My dear, I'm just going out now," said Beatrice, popping her head into Curt's room.

"Okay. Oh, and thanks for letting me stay here. I really appreciate it."

"Yes, my pleasure. And here are the keys so you can come and go without bothering the porter." She handed Curt two keys in a leather pouch. "Oh, what about a meal? Goodness. And dinner tonight?"

"I haven't really thought about it. I'm sure I'll just nip out and buy myself some lunch." Curt realized he was talking too loudly, because she took a step back.

"I'll cook us a little something, then, for dinner," she said, leaving the room.

"What time?" Curt called out.

But she didn't hear him.

Curt turned back to the two remaining letters, one — more correctly a package —from Jilly, and the other from Hawaii. He didn't know anyone in Hawaii. *Someone's on holiday?* He remembered the airport bar, the Hawaiian bartender. *Brah,* the bartender had said to him.

He decided to go out for food and coffee, to take the letters with him. He found a brassy pub at the end of the street where he was the only patron. Seated in the corner, coffee in hand, he opened Jilly's parcel.

Double Bay, Sydney

Curt:

Here are some copies of bills I've paid for you, bank balances and a statement of account from Jeffrey Bates. Do you know, in all the years I've known you, I've never written you a letter? We've lived so close to each other. People take on a different personality in a letter, don't you think?

Much has happened, but I'll save it until we talk. Please take good care of yourself.

Love, Jilly

He looked through the bank statements and lawyer's bill. Lastly Curt opened the letter from Hawaii.

Honolulu, Hawaii

Dear Curt,

I am no smooth talker, so I'll just come out and say it like it is.

Jilly called me today with the news of Margaret's tragic death. I am very sorry. I begged Jilly to let me know where you were so I could finally, after all these years, contact you. Now it's to pass on my condolences.

I have to say my piece, but I deeply regret it has to coincide with your mother's death.

Curt, my name is Noah Lopez. I am your father.

I can't imagine what it must be like to read those words. I wonder what your face looks like, if it looks like mine. There are so many things that have been kept from you, some of the secrets are not my place to tell. There were so many lies.

I guess you know you were adopted. How could she keep that from you? I'll bet you are a fine-looking young man.

If you'll agree, I'd like to meet you. I'd like a chance to explain. Could you come to Hawaii? There are so many things to tell you, I must do it in person. Will you think about it? I've had the money for your ticket saved for years. If you do wish to come, please contact me at the hotel address (where I work), and I'll send you a plane ticket right away.

This letter is meant to be good news in a time of grief. I hope it doesn't make things worse.

Please call or write. I still don't know how to contact you in Australia. Jilly is trying to protect you. Please come.

— Noah Lopez

"William, let's have coffee to discuss my offer." April's voice was followed by a beep.

William had been putting her, Francisco and Philip off for a while now. It had been a long day at the store.

He looked at the two pieces of mail in his hand. One a phone bill, the other from Hawaii: U.S. stamp, green pen, a man's firm, sharp handwriting. He could hear Janis walking around in the kitchen above him. She was going out with Robin that night to discuss where they were going to live now that a baby was on the way. She may sell the house.

William opened his phone bill, then the letter from Hawaii.

He went up to see Janis before she left. Explained the whole thing in fits and starts he was so excited. "I've been waiting for this forever."

He went downstairs immediately and phoned Francisco.

"No, I'm not going to call my parents. I'm just going to fax him that I'm coming and get on a plane. Besides, it's got nothing to do with them. This is about me. Probably about my brother too. This Noah, he may know where he is. Mom is really fragile now anyway. It's better this way."

Janis wished him luck, said that she'd look after everything while he was gone.

Francisco loaned him the money for the ticket, saying, "It's best not to take anything from him. It'll give you even footing when you meet. Take a few weeks. Do some thinking about it all, William. Bon voyage."

Two days later William stood at Toronto's Pearson International Airport with his suitcase in hand. As he approached the check-in counters, he looked around the concourse, its polished floors, at the people coming and going, shopping, looking tired and hungry. He checked in, smiling at the woman from the airline and slung his carry-on over his shoulder. William disappeared behind the departure gates.

Jilly left for the airport with plenty of time to spare. She'd cleaned the tiles in the bathroom, dusted the furniture, swept the kitchen floor, watered all the plants, locked the outside shed and latched all the windows. As she double-checked the front door, the only item out of place was a glass in the sink. She'd been parched when the taxi had tooted its horn, and since there had been no time to wash it she'd placed it in the sparkling sink, half an inch of water left in the glass's bottom, a crimson lipstick moon hanging from the rim.

"I'm going to Hawaii," she'd said to Kylie yesterday on the phone. "Curt phoned a few days ago. When I mentioned my trip, he said he may stop over in Hawaii on his way home. Could I pass on a message for you — if I see him?" Jilly hadn't explained *why* she was going, just that she was to visit an old friend. She and Kylie had arranged to meet at the airport the next day; Kylie had a letter for Curt.

Jilly had spoken with Kylie several times since Curt had left. They both missed him, and having this in common seemed a comfort.

The taxi pulled out of her driveway, leaving the dark-bricked house resolute, unmoved by her sudden departure.

Jilly had told no one else she was going. She'd made the reservations the day after talking to Noah. Now, suddenly, her first trip overseas in more than twenty years was upon her. She knew Curt. He'd go straight to Noah. One letter would be enough. In all likelihood William would react the same way. She *had* to explain her side of the story. Every instinct drew her to Hawaii, to the twins, to Noah.

Margaret's grey face had been expressionless when Jilly read the suicide note. She saw the note before Curt did. It was addressed to Curt, but the "You'll forgive me, I promise," *that* was meant for Jilly, she was certain of it. When she cried at the funeral, it was less because Margaret was gone than because Jilly knew she had to face her life, what she'd done, what had been done to her, what she'd given up.

While packing yesterday Jilly had dug through her jewellery box to find the silver bracelet Noah had given her. Now, in the back seat of the taxi winding through Sydney, Jilly fingered the bracelet, recalling her trip with Noah to the north of England, Blackpool, in 1966.

The summer season had ended several weeks before, so the resort was cheap and convenient. They'd be back in time for Noah's shift at the pub. It would be the last time they could say they didn't have a worry in the world.

Jilly knew she was two months pregnant, sick most mornings, but Noah had no idea. He was like a kid at the seashore in Blackpool, running on the beach, twirling her around. More often she insisted on slow walks, while he made light of the cold days, the stormy, grey English sea. He didn't really like Blackpool. It made him homesick, but still the sea put him in such a marvellous mood.

They spent the first day at the beach, walking, holding hands — she imagined Hawaii, the palm trees, blue sky, sea, paradise, a ukulele in the background. It was Blackpool's finest hour — perhaps even theirs.

That night, with the moon beaming in through the window,

she told him: she was pregnant. Directly. Firmly. There could be no misunderstanding. No jokes.

"It'll be okay. We'll manage," he'd said. "We can get married when we get back. I love you, Jilly."

She held on to that moment for three years, waiting for it to happen. *I may still be waiting*, she thought as the taxi crossed Whitlam Square heading down Wentworth Avenue.

The next day Noah disappeared for two hours. She assumed it was to avoid her morning sickness, but he came bounding into the hotel room before lunch with his hands behind his back and a smirk on his face. "I couldn't afford a ring," he said. "I found this at an antique store."

She knew he'd stolen the bracelet. He had no money. She had bought him the train ticket. She was paying for the hotel room — "Mr. and Mrs. Noah Lopez," she'd said without a flinch as she'd checked in. The clerk had looked them over, her frown of disapproval at their mixed marriage obvious.

Noah and Jilly returned to London and moved in together: a one-room flat attached to the back of a house not far from Chelsea. It was curtainless and cold, but it was all they could afford.

While she was pregnant, waiting and happy, Jilly tried to cheer the place up. She and Noah whitened the walls with the landlord's leftover paint. There wasn't enough to do the ceiling, so she had to ignore the stain above the stove. Noah had received a postcard from a friend in Hawaii. She hung it on the wall, imagining a mantelpiece below it.

The only door inside their flat led to the bathroom: a toilet and a sink. Thankfully they often had hot water. They bathed in sections or stole over to Beatrice's for a bath. Later, after the boys were born, when she became too poor, too thin to let anyone see her body up close, she closed the door and sponged herself down in private. By that time her body, once rosy and round, was only a memory.

Telling Curt apart from William was impossible at first. She was always tired, her back ached. Why had she removed their hospital bracelets? She was an awful mother. She agonized but ended up putting nail polish on the big toe of "William." A month later he started sucking his toe and the nail polish disappeared, but by that time she could tell who was who. Somehow they'd become distinct in her mind.

She shivered, her ribs stuck out, her legs were weak, the hair on her arms turned to a fine, fuzzy down. She sat on the couch and breastfed them both at once, their little bodies resting along her forearms, miniature feet wriggling in her armpits — like two footballs, Noah said.

She had stopped breastfeeding when they were fifteen months because she'd stopped producing enough milk. "Malnutrition" — a small, unfortunate by-product of her prudent frugality.

When Curt and William were toddlers, she fought to provide them with potatoes and carrots. She boiled them, mashed them up with a fork, added a bit of butter or milk when she could. They all ate it. Some nights, when there was truly nothing, she crushed ice, pretended it was ice cream and made up stories about the feasts they were going to have. They just had to stick together.

Curt's nose bled more often than not. William had perpetual diarrhea and wet the bed. They scraped by on church handouts and Noah's odd jobs. But his drug addiction deepened. He stayed away nights, hardly worked, spoke less.

Jilly came to regret every penny she spent. They were

always late paying their rent. Next year the boys would have to begin school. A teacher would be onto her in a flash. This was going to end one way or another.

Her landlord's wife sometimes gave her leftovers. "Bubble and squeak?" she'd ask through the back window. And one Christmas, near the end, she gave them thick slices of corned beef. It was generous, but it made William and Curt sick.

Four months later, on a day not unlike many others, Jilly looked at her two boys — ribs and collarbones protruding — and raged. She wrapped the boys up and walked all the way to Beatrice's in South Kensington, one boy holding each hand. She wouldn't neglect them; she wouldn't starve them to death.

After that everything changed. Her boys got enough to eat, they grew strong, but their lives, although preserved, were never the same.

As the cab drove on toward the Sydney airport, passing the open fields of Moore Park, Jilly began to reclaim herself, her history. Falling in love with Noah was the only risk she'd taken. It was the only time she'd smiled without having been asked to. She *had* something then, before Margaret stole it.

Margaret. The pretty one, the funny one, the smart one.

When Jilly arrived at the airport and stood in the long queue to check her luggage, she admitted to herself why she'd always had children around her. Over the years her students, especially her favourites, had been a kind of compensation. And a few years ago she'd wanted to become a foster parent. But she must have known deep down they'd never be enough.

Margaret had talked her out of it anyway. "How many children can one woman let go?" she'd said.

"You bloody bitch," Jilly had spat back.

It was the only time she stood up to Margaret in thirty years. It felt good, but the consequences were severe. Curt had left home and moved in with Kylie. Margaret manufactured a depression. Injuring Curt was her trump card against Jilly and she played it with devastating force.

Jilly checked her luggage and sat on a bench outside the airport.

Kylie arrived, her makeup running a little, her work clothes rumpled. Jilly's heart went out to her. Then, suddenly, Jilly realized Kylie would want, would need her blessing. She would matter to someone. They hugged.

As Kylie pulled away from her, she placed a letter for Curt in Jilly's hand.

"I'll give it to him," Jilly said. "I promise." Then she turned and walked into the airport, leaving Kylie there alone.

How to get from *knowing the truth* to *telling the truth*? Jilly was a woman with greying hair, a youngish face, who had given up everything but was about to lay claim to what had been lost. She tried to remember their favourite childhood poems, early stories, tidbits, anecdotes, Battersea Park, their last meeting. Her boys, her beautiful boys.

On Christmas Day at Margaret's, 1972. Curt had been sitting on the floor in front of Jilly. Margaret was in the kitchen checking the bird in the oven. It was one of the first times Margaret allowed her to see Curt since London, and now he was almost six.

"I miss you," Curt whispered, his voice carrying the last trace of a British accent.

It was as if Jilly heard it without seeing his lips move. Her heart leaped. She had so desperately wanted to say, *I miss you too.*

Curt was playing with her bracelet when he said it. She wanted to hold him, press down the dark tuft of hair standing up on the crown of his head. She wanted to feel the weight of his body against hers. She wanted to smell on him the scent of dirt and wrestling, running and playing. But Jilly did not, could not. She didn't respond. She had signed the adoption papers.

With her silence, she rejected him. The memory rendered false in his young mind and the secret that had almost wriggled out of her mouth was reburied. If she'd snapped, scooped him up and held him, she might have broken Margaret's spell. She'd never worn the bracelet since then. Until today.

It was Jilly — not Margaret — who was the first to consider suicide. William and Curt were almost four years old. She'd run out of ways to trick herself. She was alone in London and had nothing left. Noah was low and fading.

She hated herself for bringing them into this world. She'd written to her father for a little "top up" money, but she couldn't bring herself to tell him, anyone. *Why hadn't she asked someone else for help?*

Noah, like a baby himself, slumped there in the corner of the flat, smacking, needle in his arm, paradise regained. By the end he was the memory of a man, often incapable of making it to the shop for bread, to the pub across London to get more. She'd forgone buying food to give him money for a fix, not that it lasted very long.

On the last day, in Battersea Park, when Noah had played with the boys, he sang them a song. What was it? Jilly couldn't quite remember. He'd given himself a short haircut, a last-ditch effort to get her to stay. She could barely walk she was so weak and exhausted. She sat on a bench, watching the boys on the swings. Noah pushed them. It was the first time she'd seen him up and about in weeks. They ran in little circles, their bony arms and legs having already gathered new strength from their short time at Beatrice's. When Ruth, Margaret and Beatrice arrived, Margaret shouted insults at Noah, but he didn't notice her, and the boys looked on confused.

There among the trees, Jilly had started to cry, deep heaving sobs. And then the boys started crying because their parents were upset. Noah was coming off something and needed more. He started to shiver. She was barely able to stand, she had so little strength, Margaret and Ruth had only allowed her to go — to say goodbye to him, to let him see the boys one last time — if she promised to eat. Anything.

They hugged together tightly, the boys crying, their arms around their parents' legs. Noah said, "I love you, baby. Don't go, baby. We'll fix it. I'll fix it." And Jilly said, "Your skin is so pale," and she touched his cheek. A seagull squawked overhead. One of the twins mimicked his father in his small, worried voice, "We'll fix it, I'll fix it." She slipped her parents' Australian address into Noah's pocket.

Ruth took William's hand, who always liked to sit on her

knee, and Margaret picked up Curt, because he was rowdier and she could discipline, and then they helped Jilly into the car. They drove away, leaving Noah with his head down. She left him for dead.

After Battersea Park they had ceased to be.

The flight home to Australia almost killed Jilly. She moved back into her parents' home, begged her father to send Beatrice money "for rent she still owed" to be used to buy Noah a one-way plane ticket to Hawaii. *Take him to the airport yourself Beatrice*, she wrote. *Put him on the plane.*

Jilly and Noah exchanged many letters early on. They talked of her visiting Hawaii, plans for him to come to Australia, but it never happened.

"He must have stolen the money for the ticket to get back there," Margaret said when Jilly told her Noah had written to her from Hawaii. That was a year and a half after Battersea Park. Margaret phoned Ruth in Canada to get a second opinion. "Oh, yes," she said after the call, "Ruth thinks he must have stolen the money too."

Ruth had returned to Canada with William to marry her "sweetheart," Roger. He had waited five years for her to come home. "Now that's a man for you," Margaret had said. Ruth had sent Jilly pictures of William growing up: in a puffy red snowsuit, on vacation at Disney World. Jilly kept them in a shoebox under her bed along with a lock of hair.

Margaret wouldn't let Jilly see Curt until she got better. "It'll be an incentive to get well," she'd said, and Jilly believed her. It took almost two years, but by that time Margaret had already legally adopted Curt. She made Jilly sign the papers while she was still sick. It was the only solution, Margaret had said. Jilly didn't remember signing her name, signing her boys away. She didn't remember anything from that first year in Australia. She was in hospital on and off, trying to remember how to eat, trying to remember how to want to live.

By the time she was on the mend, Margaret had changed her mind. Jilly would not be getting the boys back. "Don't tell him, Jilly. If you love him, you won't tell him. For his sake. We'll call you Aunt Jilly." Given the state Jilly was in at the time, she actually thought she was very fortunate to be allowed to see him at all, to be offered a role.

For the next year Margaret continued to beat her down, saying, "You're not stable, Jilly. That's why I took him. Besides, I've put too much work into this now. It's best for Curt. And William. Ruth fully agrees." Jilly was never sure if Ruth was wholly on Margaret's side. She didn't know what or who to believe. Margaret was unwavering and calculated. "This is how it is going to be. No one will ever tell them, Jilly. They must have a chance to recover from what you've done to them." For a time, Jilly convinced herself that it was for the best, that it was all her fault.

Once, while Curt was in the midst of a teenage crisis, Margaret said to Jilly, "He rebels because of you, you know, not me." She meant it as a slight, but she had it all wrong. It made Jilly feel legitimate.

Jilly had stayed by Margaret's side to be near Curt. How could she not? Yet she and Margaret never repaired their relationship. "Her best friend for years" the reverend said, introducing Jilly at the funeral, but she had felt chained to her. Margaret hadn't openly threatened to tell Curt the truth, but Jilly knew she was always in Margaret's sights, her finger never far from the trigger. Jilly paid her price, day by day.

She wondered now if Noah was married. He wasn't seven years ago when he sent his last letter. It said "Still haven't found anyone as perfect as you Jilly." He always could blanket her in flattery.

She thought that the boys would have been all right if they had stayed together; they knew how to look after each other. In London, the boys used to talk to each other in their own private language. Only the other knew what was being said. They had been inseparable.

She'd tried so hard for so long. That's what no one acknowledged; no one remembered how long she'd lasted, how strong she'd been to keep the family together.

The plane began its descent into Honolulu International Airport. *Noah, my love, I'm here.*

PART II

On the beach Jilly laid her head on Noah's chest. She rested there while Noah fell asleep on the sand.

They'd spent the afternoon by the palm trees, eating red-and-yellow shaved ice in a cup, looking out at the waves. In a quiet voice, she asked him about the drugs, how he'd gotten off them. The truth was that sometimes she'd helped him to shoot up. Prepared it for him, helped him find a vein. He'd *needed* her.

Noah must have known she'd ask this. It was inevitable. He raised his chin up and said, "I've never touched them on the island and I haven't left since 1971. I'm safe here."

They went to visit an old friend of Noah's.

"He's not here Noah. He's at Waimea," said a woman at the door.

Noah borrowed a long, white surfboard from the garage and strapped it to the roof of his car and then drove to Waimea Bay. The surf was like nothing Jilly had ever imagined. She sat on the beach a long way back, watching him paddle out. After a time she couldn't make him out at all.

She dozed off as the afternoon wore on, still jet lagged, and when she woke up Noah appeared walking out of the water and up the beach with an older man. They smiled at her from a distance. She stood.

"Dad, this is Jilly." The old man smiled.

"It's nice to meet you," she said, a little stunned, wondering how she looked, having just woken up and with no lipstick on.

Noah's father nodded at her. He was barrel-chested, brown and weathered. She thought his eyes danced the same way Noah's did. After a few moments he patted Noah on the shoulder twice, smiled at Jilly once more, and walked off.

Noah was wet, standing close to her now, the salt caking in his eyebrows. "He told me I'm too old to be surfing out there. I only got one wave. Too hard on my old bones." Noah paused, squinting back out at the surf. "I haven't done that, surfed in the middle of the day, in years."

He'd dug the board straight up into the sand and without hesitating gently pulled her into him.

Hawaii. This man. Noah. They picked up from where they'd left off in Blackpool so many years ago. No time had passed; no love lost. His skin, brown in the evening light, felt the same to her fingers, his breath on her neck.

They stood looking out at the sea, darkness falling as they pressed together. "Stay," he said. "Please stay. Here, with me."

Jilly looked down at her bracelet, bright silver on her wrist. He still made her laugh, still blanketed her in flattery, was still both gentle and impenetrable. But here, he fit the landscape. He was a part of the volcanic rock, the coarse green grasses, the intoxicating equatorial flowers, the lush vegetation, the deep blue corduroy ocean, the soaring sea birds, the abrupt mountains, the hard flat horizon.

Jilly turned and looked at Noah before she answered. His head was down. He was taking slow, measured steps, hands behind his back. They'd gone on a morning walk before his shift. The late-winter sun was warm, brighter than it was hot. "Curt and William are connected." They stopped to rest on a park bench. Before them the sea reached all the way out to the sky.

"But both arriving the same day? Only hours apart?" said Noah, following the horizon, checking for clouds. "I think it's a good sign."

"Identical twins have a bond that forms early on, perhaps even before they're born. They share everything." Jilly patted Noah's cheek. "Don't confuse hope with fate, Noah. This is neither."

He didn't respond. He'd already confessed to having limited memories of the boys' first years in London. She looked off in the other direction, at Diamond Head. Noah and Jilly had been together every moment since she met him in the hotel lobby wearing a yellow dress, lipstick and her new sandals.

Noah had taken Jilly to his favourite places and they'd begun to fill in the gaps. She had compressed so many memories, so much pain, confusion and regret into her life, that those London years now seemed equal to twice their weight. Despite the strain, she decided everything must be discussed, said aloud, to make sure it was real, for them both.

"After Battersea Park nothing remained as it was. Ruth booked a flight to Canada and packed William's things in her suitcase. Her hair wasn't done properly that morning. She kept repeating that Roger was to meet her at the airport in Toronto. They were going to look after William until I was on the mend. Margaret had decided — had fixed — everything.

"Margaret rung my father early one morning and he wired me money. My parents never knew about the boys, ever. Margaret bought the plane tickets. She was to travel with Curt and I was to follow in two weeks. 'Don't you dare get cross with me, Jilly,' she'd said. 'I wasn't the one who got us into this.'

"I remember the rain on the morning Ruth and William left for Canada, can still see it bouncing off the black cab waiting outside Beatrice's flat. Ruth had William by the hand. I was standing behind Margaret, wrapped in a blanket. It was cold. I'd already given William a final hug in the kitchen, smoothed down the dark hair on the crown of his head. Curt stood in front of Margaret, her hand clamped down on his head, but when Ruth turned and opened the front door of the cab the boys sprang forward and clung to each other. In that moment, no one moved.

"'Now that's quite enough,' Margaret said and she stepped forward and separated them, putting William's hand back into Ruth's and shuffling them into the cab. I'll never forget William's face, tears, low in the cab's window, staring back at me, at his brother, quizzical and accusatory at the same time."

It seems so obvious to Jilly, sitting next to Noah on this park bench after so many years, that she continued to think of him as a young man, the young Noah who she left standing with his head down in Battersea Park. He had been profoundly disoriented back then. It was as if London had forced him to live without gravity. When drugs took over she convinced herself that they were what kept him from returning to Hawaii, from leaving her.

Noah looked away from the horizon. "I'm glad you stayed last night," he said, pressing his lips together.

Jilly recognized Curt in his expression. "I'm glad I stayed too," she said and reached over to take his hand in her own.

They had gone to dinner at a restaurant on the beach and the softly focused night unfolded slowly. She'd felt distant, as if she watched it as a movie rather than participated in it. Noah's strong gaze gently panning down her neck, tenderly directing her to the shore for an after-dinner walk, to talk by the sea, to taste the ocean on his lips, to gaze at a moon as white as coconut fruit. And so it was. After twenty-three years apart, with the Pacific Ocean lapping at their sand-covered toes, in one swift take Jilly had let Noah pull her into his arms, his life.

How much and how little had changed.

He cured her timidity, he softened her will. She enjoyed the sensation of being desired, held by Noah's gaze. Neither of them had married and that was in itself almost enough for her as she tripped into the lobby, the elevator, the doorway, his bed. They fell asleep in each other's arms, her head on his chest. It might have been London. The year might have been 1966. She might have been young again.

Jilly and Noah left the bench where they were sitting and walked back across the park toward the hotel, stopping at a shop where Jilly bought Noah a new shirt.

At the hotel Noah agreed to meet her for an early dinner. They had to devise a plan. He agreed. How were they to break it to the boys? Slowly if possible. But they must make sure they had the same story, the same tempered regard for Margaret and, to a far lesser extent, for Ruth. They had to prepare.

"I can't believe they're really coming," he said, taking her hand.

The plane's cabin was dark. Beside Curt a passenger slept. The lights on the wing flashed in a steady rhythm. He wasn't sure if the sun was about to rise or set. *The fine hair on Kylie's arms. Bread and eggs fried in olive oil, washing it all down with beer. The smell of lemon wood polish. The light resistance of piano keys, half notes.*

William's plane was almost empty. He couldn't sit still, fidgeting, walking up and down the aisles, stretching his legs. He took out a pen and some paper, wrote *Dear April.* He tried to find words to explain a secret that he'd kept too long. No opening line seemed adequate and he couldn't focus. In the plane's small window, he caught a glimpse of his reflection. *It's finally happening.*

By getting on this plane, heading to Hawaii, to Noah, Curt knew he had chosen a direction. Was it his past he was heading toward, or was he just a part of other people's pasts — the result of their mistakes, the source of their guilt? The cure manifested itself as the curse and suddenly language and thought only made him feel worse. Sightlessness. Dreams. Oblivion. Curt longed to be relieved.

William looked down at the backs of his hands. Turned them over palms upward, put them together as if in prayer, opened them as if miming a book, curled his fingers into fists. The plane was a projectile, firing him toward his destination. It couldn't happen fast enough. He was eager for answers. The Pacific Ocean was too large, the plane too slow.

Heroically Curt tried to force himself to sleep. His body ached. Outside, in a sublime reversal, the sun rested below the clouds in a perspective once reserved only for God. Loneliness swept over him in a shiver and the orange light faded; he dreamed of himself as a boy, playing blind-man's buff, an itchy tartan scarf tied around his head, over his eyes. It was summer and there were children about. He was lurching with outstretched arms, laughing but afraid. Each step along a precipice. All eyes were on him, while his own were blinded. *It's just a game*, he tells himself.

In the hubbub in the hotel's lobby, two diligent porters were going about their work, trying to ignore a three-year-old who was having a temper tantrum and her mother's efforts to conciliate her. Conferencing bankers in assertively casual pants strolled by as the mother issued ultimatums. A tray of forks in the café off the lobby crashed to the floor and snapped the child out of it.

The previous night, when William checked in — three hours after Curt — the front-desk clerk put him on the same floor, two rooms apart, just as Jilly and Noah had planned. "Close but not too close," they'd reasoned. "It'll be late. They'll stay in their rooms. We'll let them sleep after their long flights and get together in the morning."

At Jilly's suggestion Noah scribbled two notes, one to be delivered to each room. *Meet me in the lobby at 9 a.m. Glad you arrived safely — Noah.*

But neither Curt nor William intended to be caught off guard the next morning and each descended on the lobby early — William almost an hour premature, Curt some ten minutes.

William tried to block out the noise in the lobby and review the facts as he scoured the vicinity. *Noah Lopez*, thought William, *should be in his fifties, darkish skin, dark eyes. He'll look a little like me. I'll recognize him when I see him surely.* William had both Noah's note and the original letter of summons in his pocket. Proof.

Like William, Curt also went down the lobby anticipating a confrontation with a much older version of himself.

Sitting in a high-backed wicker chair, William had a full view of all possible routes in and out of the lobby. He observed a squeaky-clean gentleman in smart shoes take the arm of his well-preserved wife.

Curt stepped off the elevator. He didn't register anything unusual, because he thought he was the only one there. Travellers milled around, wandered about the lobby checking in, checking out.

Through crowds of people rushing to catch tour buses, newlyweds scurrying to get a good spot on the beach, retirees enroute to the café to claim their free continental breakfast, William instantly recognized Curt. "Excuse me?" said William throwing his voice over the throngs.

Curt looked around, saw William, their eyes locked.

"Noah," said William. "Lopez." He exaggerated his words. It was as if he was lip-synching himself. "Looking for Noah Lopez?"

"Yes," managed Curt as he waded against a small current of children.

Then they were facing each other.

"I ..." Curt began and then trailed off.

Humanity raged around them. For a brief moment, they were the eye of the storm.

"My name is Curt."

"You don't remember me," said William.

They shake hands. The fit was precise.

"And you are?" Curt added.

William was struck dumb.

At that moment the elevator doors opened behind them and Jilly and Noah stepped out.

"No! No! This is not how it was supposed to be." Jilly was upset, covering her eyes.

Noah held her by the arm.

"Jilly? What the ... what ...?"

"Are you Noah?"

"Let's all go and sit down." Noah held Jilly more firmly.

"Is this some kind of joke?"

"Curt, I wanted to tell you. I'm sorry, I just ..."

"What are you doing here, Jilly? What's going on?"

"How about breakfast?"

"Jilly, who are these people ... who are you?"

Since it was early the café was only partially full. The low tables were pushed closely together and several plastic palm trees formed a loose canopy above the patrons. Large photographs of Hawaiian beaches hung on the walls.

"It wasn't supposed to happen like this. We wanted to explain. Ease you into it."

"Are you my father, then?"

The families sitting at the larger tables were on holidays from Wollongong or Hamilton or Pittsburgh or Dortmund. The fathers were heavyset and wore open-necked shirts. They seemed to be adding up how much the breakfast was going to cost. "Can anyone tell me if toast is extra?" The mothers at the tables around them had on comfortable clothing, "It is going to be a long bus ride around the island today," they said. They'd packed snacks for their children, who were either playing with their food or slyly ordering more. In either case their mothers knew full well it was annoying their fathers.

"… that's when we all separated. It was never supposed to be forever. You'd both just become Margaret's and Ruth's so quickly. Margaret felt it was best."

Curt was finding it hard to stay focused on the details or faces around him: his new brother, father, mother. His mind wandered instead to his mother's flat, its solid sandstone blocks, its view across Sydney harbour. He couldn't believe what he was hearing. He crunched on the ice at the bottom of his orange juice.

"I think it's strange that I remember you, but you don't remember me," said William. "But children's minds are … well, maybe you suppressed it? The memory, I mean. It must have been traumatic for us at the time."

"More coffee?" the waiter asked, appearing suddenly. After refilling their cups he drifted across the café to the "oohs" and "ahs" from tourists eating guava and papaya for the first time.

"I don't understand. Why didn't Mum ever tell me any of this?"

"You tell them. You should tell them," said Jilly, motioning to Noah, who hadn't said anything.

"Back then things were different. When I went to England, I was young. I made mistakes. I hurt people. I hurt Jilly. I'm the one who did this — "

"That's not all true," interrupted Jilly. "It was both of us. We tried so hard to make it. Curt, you met Beatrice? Well …"

At the table next to them, a young boy refused to sit still. His father was almost shouting at him. They were on holidays for "all of us to enjoy ourselves." His wife asked him to please lower his voice because she was "sure other people could hear." The boy sat still after that.

"I can't believe Mom didn't tell me. She knew all this all along?" said William. "She's not very well at the moment, you know." He paused, taking a sip of his coffee, smiling.

Curt lit a cigarette.

"Noah missed Hawaii. That was part of it. Also, he didn't know how to be a father. We were young, poor and scared. Looking back on it, drugs seemed a way to get some peace. To escape."

At the next table, the young boy's father had calmed down. He was nodding to his wife. She had him by the hand, was whispering to him and he was saying "I know, honey, I know." Everyone in the café was a long way from home.

Noah's broad shoulders stooped listening to Jilly tell the whole story. Sometimes he forced an apologetic smile.

They ate breakfast, chewing and swallowing when the silences lengthened and became too uncomfortable.

Ka'ena Point was windy, but the day was clear. Noah motioned to the horizon, in the direction of the island of Kaua'i. Curt nodded, said he could see it in the distance. Ahead the trail faded to sand and, Ka'ena Point was exposed. This was their second stop on the North Shore. The trail they had been walking on ran along the rocky coastline, following a sloping mountain covered in coarse grass, mostly yellow, some patches of green.

A lot of what Noah wanted to say to William and Curt was about the ocean. The surf. The reefs. The way waves pitch and hollow out. Things his father explained to him. Elemental lessons of survival. He believed he knew things about the horizon that could make life easier for a young man.

Noah came out here, the western extremity of Oahu, once a year. He came on the anniversary of their last day together — Battersea Park. He was not sure if he had it right, the exact date, but he came anyway. It was as close to Jilly in Australia as he could manage without leaving Hawaii. Today the sea pounds. Other years it had been quiet. Sometimes there were whales.

As they approached the end of the point, Jilly loitered ten paces behind. Around them the sea swells heaved and turned. It had been a much longer walk than Noah suggested, not quite three miles. They passed a cave, a small blowhole. It'd been a long day of sightseeing, but the sight of them together was what drained her the most. It was starting to sink in. What she was regaining coupled with the unimaginable weight of what she'd forgone. Today William, his accent, his stories, his whole unknown history in Toronto were breaking upon her.

The boys were of a slighter build than their father. Noah stood with his legs farther apart, his gait was shorter, his shoulders more broad. They were taller, better proportioned, more graceful.

Noah was making waves in the air with his hands, pointing to places across the ocean, gesturing an explanation of where the swell was coming from today. The sun was low in the sky. A seagull dove into the sea. They waited for it to surface.

William sat on the remains of a fallen concrete observation tower, resting. Curt lit a cigarette, stood, inspected land's end. Jilly reached Noah and took his hand. They didn't look at each other. Instead, they looked out across the water framed by the volcanic rock — once molten and flowing, now cool and deliberate.

The seagull lifted out of the ocean, a silver fish in its beak. They watched it fly, soaring over the mountain.

"This point," begins Noah, speaking slowly. "It's also called Leina a Ka'uhane." He had his sons' attention but seemed unsure. "It means 'leaping place of the ghosts.' This is where souls of the dead leap into the next world. It's called, simply, *Po*."

It became obvious to Curt that the crushing loss of his mother had freed three people. His pain was their joy.

After days of sightseeing and talking, Jilly sensed Curt was brooding and invited him to go for a walk.

"Curt, I had to come," said Jilly, softly, taking in the golden curve of Waikiki beach.

"I know. I know," said Curt.

She looked down at her feet, toes in the sand. Then she whispered, "Are you mad at me?"

It was a few moments before Curt answered. "When I got off the plane, I kept telling myself not to get my hopes up, in case something went wrong — to protect myself, you know." He gazed at surrounding sunbathers, the smell of coconut oil hanging in the air. "Say this Noah guy turned out *not* to be my real father, or didn't show up, or was a real bastard, or wanted something. I was trying to keep my expectations low … but you … all of this."

A small crowd gathered around a volleyball net. Somewhere, not far away, Taiko drummers were giving a recital — low-grade thunder — to celebrate the blossoming of the island's cherry trees.

"In some ways I hoped I'd meet my birth father, go for a long lunch at which he'd tell me a few unmistakable things about himself, myself. Tell me that my mother died in child-birth, or that he hasn't seen her in twenty-five years, or that she's living in England and doesn't want to be contacted. I thought it could be that simple."

"We have to talk about Margaret," said Jilly. "She — "

"You've told me what happened," interrupted Curt.

The volleyball crowd went quiet, tensed up. The ball was served, bumped, set, spiked — it fell wide of the line drawn in the sand. The crowd clapped.

"I want us to be able to talk, Curt."

"Like we did on the verandah at your place? Come on, Jilly, everything you told me that day, everything you said at Mum's funeral … why should I trust you?"

Two sets of bronzed players in dark sunglasses leapt about after the volleyball. More people gathered.

"I want you to believe me," said Jilly. "Curt …" She stopped, turned away. She pressed her fist into her forehead, resting her elbow on her knee.

"How do you think I feel?" asked Curt.

"I know. I know. I'm sorry, Curtis." Jilly's voice trailed off into a whisper.

Curt could see she was crying. "Don't call me Curtis," he finally said, quietly. He couldn't help it. It was what he was thinking. "You know that's what Mum called me."

"But I'm the one who gave you that name …" She turned away from him, averting her eyes.

"I don't want to talk about this anymore," he said.

More people had gathered around them. It was not the right place to hold this conversation. Curt and Jilly could no longer see the game from where they were sitting.

They sat for a long time in silence. The game ended and the crowd began to disperse. In a few moments, where there had been a wall of people, there lay ocean, horizon and sky.

"Curt. I know you loved her, but you have to believe the truth about your mother. It's the only way you'll ever begin to forgive her for what she's done. Look at what you've gained. A brother. A twin brother. Curt, the times I wanted to tell you ..." Her throat sounded raw, gasping, pathetic.

Curt looked at her, cringed at the sight of the grey part in her hair. Was this really just about *her* missed chances?

He sifted sand through his fingers, trying not to let the torrent of emotions register on his face. But it was no use. He saw his mother, sunken into that chair, her glazed face, the gin dribble down the front of her tennis frock.

Jilly had spoken about their past, about London, Margaret, Ruth, Beatrice, about Noah's addiction, about her own final decision to go for help, about the walk across London right into his mother's trap, and throughout her story Jilly had apologized. She seemed to regret not having been strong enough to combat his mother, the woman who'd made him sandwiches and sent him off to school, who'd stroked his head and helped him learn the piano, who'd sung him lullabies, *o-ver the sea to Skye.*

Curt stood up, brushing the sand from his shorts and said, "Let's go back. I want to go back to the hotel." Then, "You didn't know her like I did. She loved me."

The tourist market engulfed William in people and gaudy colours.

"How much is that?" he asked. The man at the jewellery stand flipped over the tag on the jade, a fine, interlocking weave fastened to a silver necklace.

"Thanks," William said and smiled. Too expensive.

Earlier, when Noah mentioned he had to work that afternoon, William assumed that he, Curt and Jilly would visit more sights together, but when Jilly had said in a private moment "Would you mind terribly if Curt and I spent some time alone this afternoon?" he responded, "Of course not."

As he wandered, William remembered the tour at the pineapple-canning factory yesterday.

"Labourers came to Hawaii from all over the world to harvest the fruit crops. Wave upon wave of immigration came to the shores of Hawaii throughout the twentieth century," the guide had said.

William desperately wanted to ask Noah about his own parents. Lopez. Spanish? Portuguese? Puerto Rican? That would be the father's side. He thought of April for a moment.

He turned a corner and wandered aimlessly into a stall. He held a T-shirt up to his chest. "Hang Loose" it said in pink-neon script.

People on holidays looked to be happiest when shopping for those they most desperately wanted to escape from: a tea towel for an incapacitated relative left at home, a bottle of tri-coloured sand for a boss, a postcard of a tropical mountain they haven't actually visited for a gullible friend. Later, back in their hotel rooms, they'll scribble on the back "Wish you were here!"

William bought a Portuguese pastry from a woman at a small shop, much like the ones he frequented on Bloor Street. He imagined home, April, Francisco, but couldn't think about making decisions. Thinking about his life back home seemed foolish, maybe even irrelevant. He could leave it all behind. Move to Australia or Hawaii. Anything could happen now ... now that he knew who he was, knew his family.

William wandered away from the market along the streets. Here and there the cherry trees were in bloom and in the distance he heard Taiko drummers. He walked toward them. *Delicious day.*

Down at the beach, a crowd of people gathered at a volley-ball game. William couldn't get very close, but he saw the ball rise into the air and guessed by the cheering of the crowd when a point had been won or lost. After the game ended and the crowd dispersed, William saw Curt and Jilly sitting on the sand, deep in conversation. He retreated to a safe distance, observing them from behind a tree.

Curt was upset. His brother's hands strained sand through his fingers, his head was down. Jilly looked defeated and wasn't saying much. The conversation had broken down.

William watched as Curt and Jilly stood and began to walk back down the beach. He followed. As he arrived at the place where they had been sitting, he stared at the two separate impressions left in the sand. He turned and headed back toward the market, to the jewellery stall, to the necklace.

"So here we all are. Noah, Jilly and the twins. The Lopezes," Curt said in the lobby that night.

Noah, Jilly and William stared at him.

"I'm going to bed," he announced.

As he climbed between the starchy sheets, he was surer than ever that one version of the truth had gone to the grave with his mum.

William got out of the pool and was handed a towel by the attendant. *He is a little taller than I am. A little thinner too. He eats spaghetti with a fork and spoon. He holds his knife like a pencil. He doesn't like salt. Has four sugars in his coffee.*

"You should have come in. It was great." William stood beside Curt, towelling down his legs, trying to get the water out of his ears. "Hey, there's a cool bar down the beach. Wanna grab a drink?"

"No," he answered and walked off.

"Okay, hand me that line," said Noah suddenly. "William, we're going to turn."

William was confused, the sail loosened. "Which one?" he said, apologetically.

Noah lurched forward to grab the rope. William tried to move out of the way. Curt felt the boat begin to struggle, and then it suddenly leaned high out of the water, standing up on one hull.

When Curt crashed into the water, his head struck the boom, not hard, but as he spun around underwater, with a mouthful of sea, thinking of his cigarettes now wet in his pocket, he raged. He managed to get upright and pulled himself above the water, gasping. The other two had already surfaced. *My lighter*, he thought and shoved his free hand into his pocket. The lighter was gone.

"Everyone okay?" asked Noah.

They'd been moving quite fast on account of the brisk wind. William had been watching a seagull that had landed in front of them in the water, squawking, bobbing. As they'd drawn closer, it had taken to the air, diving, swerving off into the distance. Curt had been thinking of Coogee, of Kylie. Jilly had passed on a letter from Kylie on the first day. She'd written that she wanted to "sort things out" when he returned. He'd also been thinking about Rachel. Not about Mallorca but about going to Scotland, about why he'd done it. That's when Noah had asked William for the rope.

Following Noah's instructions they flipped the boat right side up and climbed back on. With the sail perpendicular to the boat, it became taut again, filling with the breeze.

"Sorry, guys," Noah said as they began to move.

Curt and William crawled forward and sat closer to the front of the boat. The twin hulls before them surged through the blue water, the sun overhead, the horizon at their arching backs, the beach dead ahead. Curt got out his cigarettes. Soaking. There was silence except for the sound of the water rushing beneath them. A small wave from a passing boat hit them side on and Curt almost fell in again. William grabbed him by the arm — steadied him.

"Thanks," said Curt.

As the beach loomed, the sun was warm and the wind was light.

Curt turned to William, still shaking a little from his near fall, from the chill of the wet clothes. "My lighter slipped from my pants when I fell in," he said. *A Love Supreme. The drain, the chewing gum.* Curt imagined it in slow motion as it fell from his pocket, sinking gold, shimmering for a split second like a fishing lure, then out of sight as the catamaran sailed on. He was never careful enough with it, with her.

Lying face up, mesmerized by the streaks of red and green and gold in the sky above Kapiʻolani Park, Curt missed the shuffling signs that the others were ready to leave. They had walked here together to watch the kites fly in the annual festival.

"We're going to head back," said Noah finally.

"But you're free to stay a while. We could meet later at the rooftop restaurant for dinner," Jilly suggested.

"Seven o'clock," added Noah.

"I'll see you then," said William, giving his brother a nod.

The three of them walked away, leaving Curt supine, the colours crisscrossing in the open sky.

A large kite made of boxes strung together had a dragon painted on its underside. It seemed to be heading somewhere as it twisted and turned at new and sharper angles to gain ground, as if trying to outsmart its master using updrafts, peaked bends, swoops. Curt regarded its owner, a small man who stood across the park. The man was wearing a dark blue T-shirt and pulled all the strings himself; without his guidance the kite would have fallen limp to the ground.

Curt turned his head to the horizon and watched sea birds soar over the ocean. The sun was becoming less hot and serious with each passing minute. He listened to the members of a family — the mother trying to get her youngest daughter to eat. The father laughed, tossing an older girl in the air.

As the sun fell behind a cloud and the dragon kite fell into shadow, Curt made a decision.

"I'm sure Curt'll be here soon," said William.

"He must still be jet lagged," offers Jilly unconvincingly, reaching forward and touching William's forearm on the table.

William looked down at her hand on his brown skin, didn't move his arm. He sat on one side of the table across from Noah and Jilly. William looked up and saw Diamond Head in the distance. It looked as if it had a halo. Then his eyes drifted over to the door. Curt was half an hour late.

"Worked at this hotel for twenty years," said Noah.

They had a window table with a view of the last few minutes of sunset, the beach, the sea. Noah was wearing a Hawaiian shirt. His fingers found the gold chain around his neck and began to twirl the shark's teeth, pressing the points into his fingertips slightly.

"You and Curt have the same laugh," said Jilly, her eyes are on the door. "Same pitch, don't you think? But you use chopsticks in your right hand, Curt is left-handed. And you cross your arms in opposite ways — you're left over right, Curt vice versa."

"Is that true?" said William. He glanced around the restaurant. "Do you think I should go look for him?"

"Let's just eat." Noah motioned for the waitress.

Suddenly, there was ukulele fanfare, and torches were lit. They turned to face the centre of the restaurant, where an

Asian chef wearing a tall paper hat was sharpening two long knives: silver blades and white bone handles glinted in the firelight. He began carving up a golden, dripping pig to rounds of applause from the restaurant patrons.

Their waitress was Hawaiian. She wore a lei of crimson and white blossoms. "The pig," she announced, "is a *kalua* pig, cooked in an underground oven — the *imu*. It is wrapped in banana leaves."

They ordered dishes of *opakapaka*, *uhu* and *kalua* pig.

William studied Noah's face, his features. They were like his own in some ways. His skin was darker, his hair had the same texture. His fingernails had the same curve.

Finally William said, "I think I'll look for Curt back at his room. Just to make sure everything's all right."

"That's fine," said Jilly. "We'll see you tomorrow, then."

Sitting alone in the piano bar, Curt began a letter to Kylie. *It's so easy for William. This is what he's been waiting for.* His mind wanders off, imagining the day when he'll be able to tell her in person.

You'll forgive me, I promise.

His mother cut out, her shadow forever cast there.

A Love Supreme.

The great curved verandah.

The creeping wisteria.

A Sydneysider.

A twin. Twins. Me and my brother. My brother and I. Us. A pair. A set.

"The twins."

Identical.

Identity.

I.

William took the elevator first to their floor, where he knocked on Curt's door, then downstairs to the lobby to check with reception. No messages. Not knowing where to look next, he wandered into the piano bar for a drink. At one of the tables sat Curt.

"Can I join you?" said William as he sat down across from Curt in a matching wicker chair.

"How was dinner?"

"It was hard without you there. They're trying …"

The bartender approached. "Would you fellas like a night cap?"

They ordered two glasses of port.

When the drinks arrived, Curt went over to the baby grand. No one in the bar seemed to mind his impromptu performance. As he began to play, he could hear his band in the back of his mind, how they worked together. Curt hunched up over the shiny piano, twisted his head around half expecting to see his drummer, but it was only William.

He played a version of the new counterpoint progression he'd been working on since Mallorca. Then he remembered how Kylie had nodded, and how he'd waved goodbye as he walked out of the bar into the Sydney night.

That night Curt had played … he was trying to remember *what* he'd played. Looking up he saw that William had a piece of paper and was drawing something.

Curt was stalling, not knowing where to go next, he was filling the room with airy jazz chords that hovered across the bar but went nowhere, which he felt was also true of himself. He began to hum, to think of a note slightly before playing it and this momentum, these decisions, grew into a groove. He was going home to Sydney.

His mind drifted inside the tune. The songs he'd been writing, their dark rhythms, modulating in open spaces, were not in love with Spain or England or America. His music, he knew now, belonged to Australia.

William studied Curt at the piano, his head bent. He would begin the image with a fragment, a part of a whole that no one else saw. Beautiful. Without boundaries. Mine. Ours.

William's arms were outstretched; the music drove him on. He needed to draw. He was as good as his brother. William heard Francisco's voice, revealing the true subject of April's portrait, *You're in every single line. Look harder.* Now he stared at the blank page wanting to draw the first lines of a sketch of Curt at the piano.

Curt finished playing. The applause snapped William out of his trance and he folded up the untouched piece of paper and slipped the failed attempt into his pocket as Curt walked over to him. "Bravo," said William before spontaneously stepping forward and embracing him. As they held each other for the first time, Curt's eyes closed. His lips pressed together in a thin line, his fists clenched.

The bar was silent, the door closed. The dark wood surrounded them. There were only a few small lights on as they sipped on their port.

"There's a phenomenon called vanishing twin syndrome," said Curt. "It happens when the mother loses one twin early in pregnancy. Often before she even knows she's pregnant, much less having twins. Kylie and I watched a documentary about it last winter. I remembered it yesterday suddenly." He looked directly at William.

"Yeah, I've heard of it. I think I've read every book there is about twins."

Curt glared. "Well, that's because *you* knew." He spat this at William, his voice suddenly sharp. He looked down, brushing imaginary crumbs off his shirt. "I don't feel what you do."

"What are you saying?"

Curt recognized William's face. The weather changed, a storm of fear swept across it. The same uncontrollable upper-lip twitch he has when he's upset.

"Curt, I'm your brother. I can help you. We can help each other."

"I'm leaving tomorrow, back to Sydney," said Curt, reaching forward, lighting a cigarette, inhaling deeply. "I have no choice. I'm really on the brink here. Jilly, Mum, you."

"You can't."

"I have to."

"I've waited my whole life for this." William looked away and then his head snapped back. "Don't be so selfish. There are two other people upstairs who have risked everything to bring us together."

"What were you expecting? One big happy family? He was a drug addict and she was too bloody stupid to leave him. She almost starved us to death. If it wasn't for my mum —"

"We might have made it."

"We might have died of malnutrition."

"We might have stayed together."

"Bullshit. Bullshit. You never knew my mother. She was always there for me …"

"I'm not saying that it's *all* her fault."

"You don't know what really happened. Jilly's only told us her side."

"You don't believe them? You think Noah and Jilly would make this up? How could anyone make up something like this?"

Curt didn't answer. Instead, he flicked his cigarette on the side of the ashtray, overzealously, and the glowing end almost fell off.

"Curt. I didn't …" William paused and looked at the ground.

"My name is not Lopez. Never has been. We don't know bugger all about each other, or what happened, or where we're from, or anything," said Curt. "You want to believe this is real? Don't be so naïve. Our real lives are back home, not here."

"What about us? We're brothers."

"If I've meant so much to you all these years, then why haven't you tried to find me before now?"

"I just …" William's voice was hardly there. "Why can't you stay?" Tears.

"I have to go home. I miss everything there."

"I'll move. I'll do whatever it takes. Live anywhere."

He stopped because Curt was reaching forward, grabbing a napkin, pressing it to his face. Then, before William could think of what else to say, before he could formulate a stronger, more convincing argument, Curt stood up and walked right out of the room.

For a time William sat still. Across from him the empty chair. He reached into his pocket and brought out the jade necklace.

Curt leaned against the back of the elevator. He exited on the seventh floor and staggered down the hallway to his room. He took off his clothes and lay on his bed. Above him on the ceiling was a mirror. A honeymoon suite. His window was open. Ukulele music seeped in from the hotel grounds. The night was warm. He could hear the traffic below. He was tired. In the mirror his eyes ran over his chest, bumped across his ribs and slid down his legs. The weight of reflection. *Is this the right thing to do?* Then, finally, there were tears. Curt fell asleep above and below his own sea.

It's me. I'm gone.

He looked into the mirror and saw his twin, his brother lying next to him. Before him floated two knives, steel blades, white bone handles, his hands covered in sweet blood, the orange sun through the window, hot. Perfectly parallel to him, it played itself out in agony, in beauty, in reason, in passion, in heat, in space, in time, in reverse, in paint, in notes, in lovers, in mothers, in fathers, in the sun, in the moon. He stood and fell toward the window, his hands smearing red across the pane, the sun lighting it from behind. Blood on a microscope slide. The sun, an eye. "No, no … NO," he screams at the mirror, bearing down on him like history. Who was who? "Wake him, make him see!"

Curt woke up in a choking sweat. Reorientation was slow. And outside, beyond the window, beyond his room, it was dawn, nothing more than the beginning of another day.

At breakfast Curt broke the news of his impending departure to Jilly and Noah. Almost nothing was said. Jilly left the table.

Curt went back to his room to pack. He was exhausted from all the walking, the sightseeing, last night's drinks, last night's dream. He lay on the bed and reread his letter from Kylie, his thoughts ricocheting. He slept most of the day.

He ordered room service, ate, then went into the bathroom and changed into his bathing suit. His plane left in five hours. A quick swim, then he would talk to William. An olive branch. He'd been too harsh last night. Unfair. Uncompromising. He'd make it up to him.

The sun was setting, and sticky red rays streamed in through the window as Curt left his room to go down to the pool.

The last two streaks of Hawaiian sunlight joined and began their retreat across the surface of the sky. A skin of coconut oil covered the pool. A rainbow trailed Curt as he left the water. He took a mai tai from a wandering waiter. "Cheers," he said and lit a damp cigarette. The rush of smoke entered his blood, followed by a wave of rum.

As Curt's mind leaped to his mother playing *The Skye Boat Song* on the piano and the *M* on her letter; as car horns blended with the ukulele music from the hotel next door; as Curt recalled the Mediterranean morning heat blasting through the window as he fought his hangover in Mallorca; as he considered Kylie for a wife; as his plane descended toward Honolulu International Airport ready to land, ready to refuel and take him away; and as William fastened the clasp of the jade necklace around his own neck, Jilly pulled her knees into her chest and thought about Battersea Park. Elsewhere, a perfect nine-foot wave rolled beneath the surfboard of Noah Lopez while he floated out among the red rays of a sunset on the North Shore of Oahu. It was the wave he wanted, the one he had been waiting for, so essential, so beautiful, but he hesitated, and now it was gone.

On his way upstairs to William's room, still in his swimsuit, Curt rehearsed. "We were born in London. That means we're British— very distressing news for an Australian. Our father is Hawaiian. Which means we're also American. Not exactly good news for a Canadian either. Seems like we've got stakes in half the world."

Curt wrapped his towel around his neck and knocked on William's door.

"Yes?" said a stout man with a German accent.

"Oh, I'm sorry. I was looking for William. Wrong door, I guess."

"No, but this is my room. Ya."

Curt spun around checking the numbers on other doors. He was on the right floor, at the right door. "When did you check in?"

"Just two hours ago," said the man.

Oh, Christ, he's left. He's gone home first.

Sweating, hardly clothed, Curt ran down the stairs and phoned Noah's room from the lobby. They weren't back yet. They weren't supposed to meet up for another hour.

"Yes, can you tell me what time the flight for Toronto leaves tonight?" Curt checked his watch. His brother's plane would be taking off any minute. It was too late.

All this born from the local, specific, immediate truth— William was gone. By playing his own hand, he'd forced his brother's. He'd been blind.

Noah opened the taxi door for Jilly and they climbed inside. As they rolled away from the airport, she said softly, "It was a good start. It was just a beginning."

They were silent for the entire ride back to the hotel. It was dark outside. They held hands. Noah patted her knee.

Curt, Noah and Jilly had stood outside the airport. In the international departures drop-off zone, Noah suggested that they get together next Christmas in Australia. They were on the curb, Curt's backpack at his side, hurried travellers surrounding them. Jilly said she would phone William first, see exactly what happened, talk to him. Then, when the dust settled, they agreed Curt would ring him.

There in front of the terminal, Noah, Jilly, and Curt looked no different than other families dropping off loved ones. The grown son hugged the father, slapped him on the back, shakes his hand. The mother put a hand to each of her son's cheeks, her lips tense, tears pending. The son looked eager to get it over with, not uncaring, simply ready to take on what life had to offer on the other side of the departure gate. They might have been the Lopez family: from Honolulu, or Dundee, or Sydney, or Toronto, or Madrid, or Paris, or London. With a final wave, Curt shuffled through the front doors of the airport and out of Noah and Jilly's line of sight.

Once he'd checked his bag and gone through the gates, Curt glanced up at the screen. His plane was delayed. They were all hours behind schedule. His eyes ran over the departure board—Toronto: now boarding.

We forgot to ask which one of us was born first, Curt thought as he hurried past a counter toward a group of people lining up at the gate. Peering through the glass door separating boarding areas, Curt saw William in the row of passengers *(Look back, please look back)*, shuffling forward onto the gangway.

The line stopped moving for a moment. William turned and glanced back over his shoulder but the security glass was tinted from the inside, he couldn't see anything. To William facing mirrored wall, all he saw was his own reflection. But something drew him anyway. His throat burned. Then, once more, the line moved on, and William obliged, shuffling forward out of Curt's line of sight.

Their planes flew into the night in opposite directions. Some of the Pacific Ocean was in darkness.

Acknowledgements

The author would like to acknowledge the financial support of the Ontario Arts Council and the City of Toronto through the Toronto Arts Council.

As this is my first, I owe a great deal to a great many.

My appreciation goes especially to my friends: Ken Babstock, Michelle Berry, Sarah Dearing and Dominic Farrell, who, during the writing of this novel, shared insights and provided invaluable scrutiny.

Thanks also to Suzanne Brandreth, Allan Hepburn, Adam Levin, Barb Panter and Andrew Pyper who all generously read various versions and drafts along the way and gave sound advice.

A large thanks to my friends Peter Darbyshire, Scott Colbourne, Lesley Grant and Paul Vermeersch for their fine friendship and thoughtful criticism over many years. Cheers.

I'd like to thank my anonymous correspondent at the Office of Administration at Glamis Castle, Jay Johnston in London and David Leys in Sydney for their thoughts and help with odd specifics. Thanks also to all the twins I spoke to and interviewed, especially: Maggie and Beth Morgan, Lesley and

Jackie Grant, and Suzanne Zelazo. Your candour was tremendously helpful.

I would also like to mention John Bank, Christian Bök, Kate Brown, Natalee Caple, Ailsa Craig, Julian Dormon, Beth Follet, Suzanne Foreman, Patrick Hyndes, Janet Inksetter, Marnie Kramarich, Madeline Lennon, George Murray, Pamela Soper, Karen Suzuki and Reuel K. Wilson, who, at different times, either helped or forced me to think about writing, art or music in new ways; my agent, Dean Cooke, for his steady and constant support; Anne Mackrell for the laughs and sharing her wisdom; and Joy Gugeler along with all the good people at Raincoast.

I must mention three books that were important resources to me as I wrote: Bruce Jenkins's *North Shore Chronicles: Big Wave Surfing in Hawaii,* Lawrence Wright's *Twins and What They Tell Us about Who We Are,* and George Sand's memoir, *Winter in Majorca.* I was also inspired by Dr. David Teplica's many wondrous photographs of twins.

I would like to thank my mother, Jocelyn Murphy; my father, Vern Bennett; Marty and Rhys Morgan; and all the other members of my various families, especially Becky Morgan, Peter and Haley Bennett and, of course, my brother David Bennett, who, although half a world away, was with me as I wrote each and every word.

Finally, and frankly, this book would not have made it out alive if it were not for the editorial hand and emotional support of Wendy Morgan. With love, thank you, Gwen.

More Raincoast Fiction:

Slow Lightning by Mark Frutkin
1–55192–406–4 $21.95 CDN/$16.95 US

In 1936 civil war Spain, Sandro Risco Canovas is blacklisted by Franco and forced to flee the city, posing as a priest along the sacred pilgrimage route, the Saint James Way. Sandro makes his way to a secret cave near his seaside home of Arcasella, setting in motion an elaborate deception that signals a descent into darkness, dream and desire.

Kingdom of Monkeys by Adam Lewis Schroeder
1–55192–404–8 $19.95 CDN/$14.95 US

Charting the steamy jungles and murky depths of the South Seas, Schroeder's collection cunningly exposes the vestiges of colonial power in Asia, reinventing the exotic, the exquisite and the exiled while sinking into a culture luxurious in irony and intrigue.

Finnie Walsh by Steven Galloway
1–55192–377–6 $21.95 CDN/$16.95 US

Finnie Walsh is Paul Woodward's best friend, a hockey fanatic and the tragic figure at the heart of a series of bizarre accidents that alter the lives of the Woodward family in a comic tale of family, friendship, redemption and legend.

Hotel Paradiso by Gregor Robinson
1–55192–358–0 $21.95 CDN/$16.95 US

Journey Prize nominee Gregor Robinson's debut novel charts a season in the life of a thirty-something expat banker in the Bahamian outport of Pigeon Cay. He has come to the subtropics in search of exotic escape, but instead stumbles upon genteel corruption, white-collar crime, racism and murder.

Rhymes with Useless by Terence Young
1–55192–354–8 $18.95 CDN/$14.95 US

In a collection praised by *The Village Voice, Publisher's Weekly, National Post* and the *Globe & Mail*, Governor General's nominee Terence Young creates both a litany of human foibles and its sensible antidote; regret and forgiveness, suppressed desire and unleashed lust, dislocation and homecoming.

Song of Ascent by Gabriella Goliger
1–55192–374–2 $18.95 CDN/$14.95 US

Journey Prize winner Gabriella Goliger's finely honed stories recount the troubled lives of the Birnbaum family, displaced German Jews who flee Hitler but cannot escape the shadow of the Holocaust. Their uprooted existence takes them from Europe to the Holy Land to Montreal to relate a history that explores the tense dialogue between present and past.